## "I _____ Jasmine Said, Her Gaze Steady On His Face.

What could she want? His body? That tantalizing thought flitted through his mind. He'd gladly oblige, but first he'd teach her some morning-after etiquette. "I see. Is it just me, or do you see the irony in that?"

For the first time, she had the grace to look a little discomfited. Not much, just a brief shift in her gaze, a tiny clearing of the throat. But Adam possessed the secret to unlocking that composure.

"What can I do for you, Jasmine?" he asked, settling back on the desk. He folded his arms, intrigued now that his pride had been restored.

Jasmine swallowed again. "I want you to spend Christmas with me at my family's estate in Lincolnshire," she said. "As my fiancé."

Dear Reader,

Do corporate jets land at Vienna International Airport?
How do you spell *goulash?* Can you take a fiacre
(horse-drawn carriage) from the Imperial Hotel to
the Hofburg Imperial Palace? The Internet is a vital, if
time-consuming, tool for authors. It doesn't always get
it right and is open to interpretation and local custom. I
visited Vienna back in the eighties, with no room in my
backpack for a ball gown and too little money to take
in the Spanish Riding School, a lasting regret. But it
was, and is still, an enchanting city, with its Fasching,
incredible architecture and rich history.

Indulging in armchair research is no substitute for being
there. My travel bug has reawakened. Until I get back to
Austria, I hope I got most of the facts right in Adam and
Jasmine's story. If I didn't, please write and enlighten
me!

And goulash? I found five different spellings while
trawling through online Austrian restaurant menus.
All I know is, it's yummy!

Best wishes,

*Jan Colley*

# JAN COLLEY

# HIS VIENNA CHRISTMAS BRIDE

Published by Silhouette Books
**America's Publisher of Contemporary Romance**

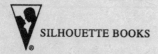 SILHOUETTE BOOKS

ISBN-13: 978-0-373-76974-2

Recycling programs
for this product may
not exist in your area.

HIS VIENNA CHRISTMAS BRIDE

**Books by Jan Colley**

Silhouette Desire

*Trophy Wives* #1698
*Melting the Icy Tycoon* #1770
*Expecting a Fortune* #1795
*Satin & a Scandalous Affair* #1861
*Billionaire's Favorite Fantasy* #1882
*Friday Night Mistress* #1932
*His Vienna Christmas Bride* #1974

---

## JAN COLLEY

lives in Christchurch, New Zealand, with Les and a couple of cats. She has traveled extensively, is jack of all trades and master of none and still doesn't know what she wants to be when she grows up—as long as it's a writer. She loves rugby, family and friends, writing, sunshine, talking about writing and cats, although not necessarily in that order. E-mail her at vagabond232@yahoo.com, or check out her Web site at www.jancolley.com.

I dedicate this book to the music of Johann Strauss II.
May you leave me in peace
now that I have written the books!

# One

Well, well, Adam Thorne thought as he lounged in his chair, staring at the woman who had just entered his office. Mohammed had come to the mountain.

Satisfaction plumped up his chest. The rugby ball he'd been tossing up and down stilled in his hands. She might have shown him the door last month after a magical night of passion, but here she was, standing in the doorway of his London office, in the flesh. He tamped down the urge to smile. She'd better be prepared to grovel, or stump up with the goods. He wasn't a man used to slights and empty promises.

"Hallo, Adam."

Taking his time, he gave the ball one last toss,

caught it, then slid his feet off the desk. "Shouldn't you be twelve thousand miles away, hard at work for my big brother?"

Jasmine Cooper, personal assistant to his brother, Nick, English but presently living in Wellington, New Zealand. Cool, composed and without doubt the most fascinating female in Adam's considerable catalogue.

"I had some leave owing."

Adam unwound his long frame, stood and skirted the desk, tossing the rugby ball into a nearby open box.

She walked toward his desk, unbuttoning her long black woolen coat, and he let his eyes have at her. She was, as usual, impeccably dressed in a navy wool trouser suit, saved from severity with a bright-yellow sweater and those four-inch spiky heels she liked. His eyes were drawn to her heels like a magnet. Years of ballroom dancing had given her the most sensational, mile-high legs. A savage bolt of desire rushed through him and his fingers twitched, recalling never-ending silky smooth skin, firm and strong as they locked around his waist, as he molded them with his hands….

"May I take your coat?"

He held out his hand while she slipped out of her coat, glancing around curiously. His office resembled a bomb site, littered with boxes. Adam was enjoying a leisurely last day as junior partner in Croft, Croft and Bayley stockbrokers. In the new year, he would be opening his own premises in the Docklands for a markedly different venture.

He slid the garment on to a hanger and turned back to her, indicating she sit. "To what do I owe this very unexpected pleasure?"

She lifted a graceful hand and patted at her long dark hair, tied back, as usual. Adam preferred it out, remembering how it tickled his chest as she straddled him, kissing his mouth. Her almond-shaped eyes, he'd discovered, interchanged between smoky gray and blue, depending on her level of arousal.

Today, she was poised and elegant, lightly made-up, the perfect milk and roses of a true English beauty with a warm, rich shade on her lovely lips. As if he hadn't been assaulted by the same sights and sounds dozens of times over the past weeks, he again recalled those eyes hazed with passion, her short, well-kept nails digging into his hips, urging him on. The desperate little panting noises that escaped her throat at the onset of orgasm, and which he just bet prim and proper Ms. Cooper was mortified about later.

Pity she'd blotted her copy book. Adam was still mightily displeased at the way she'd treated him afterward. It had taken six dates to charm her into bed, spurred on by her quietly confident decree that she would not be another notch on his crowded bedpost. He'd persevered because he was on holiday, his time was more or less his own and he'd enjoyed her company more than expected, considering she was nothing like the women he usually dated. If people had a type, Jasmine Cooper was nothing like his.

Hell, he'd persevered because she'd told him no.

"I just spoke to Nick last week," he mused. "He didn't mention you were coming over."

He'd also courted the displeasure of his brother, who seemed to take a personal interest in keeping him away from his P.A., going so far as to tell him that a woman like Jasmine wouldn't give him the time of day.

Adam never could resist a challenge, but his brother had been partly right, as it turned out. After an incredible night of unbridled passion, he'd been shown the door. She couldn't wait to be rid of him. Perhaps she considered him a lapse of her impeccable judgment, or thought he might be less than discreet and tell her boss. One moment, she'd been all over him—literally—the next, it was here's your hat, what's your hurry?

Adam was a master of keeping things casual but at least he did so with charm and good manners. This elegant woman in front of him may look genteel, with her cultured accent that would be at home in Windsor Castle, but she'd dented his normally robust esteem and he didn't like that one bit.

Now she sat in front of him, her hands clasped tightly in her lap. A second glance showed him how tightly. Her knuckles were white. An interesting show of nerves.

"I usually come home at Christmas."

Logical. It was Christmas Eve and she was English and presumably had family here. But why bother coming to see him when a few short weeks ago she couldn't wait to be rid of him?

"And you just happened to be passing?" he said dryly.

Her lips softened. "Not exactly."

Jasmine was a woman of few words. Well-educated, classy, she would never run away with her mouth—although he recalled one or two things she had done with her mouth that had caused him all sorts of pleasure. Adam put his desk between them, feeling as horny as a school kid. He'd been working twenty hours a day since returning from New Zealand, winding up his affairs here, hunting out investors, organizing new premises. He hadn't had a date since he got back. The London debutantes that usually peppered his crowd had had short shrift from him of late—and that, he told himself firmly, had nothing to do with the trouble he was having dislodging the thought of one particular woman from his mind. He only gave Jasmine Cooper a second thought because she'd pissed him off!

"I need to ask a favor," she said, her gaze steady on his face.

Adam raised a brow. That was rich. He'd asked her a favor, one that could make a huge difference to the success of his new entrepreneurial start-up business. She had promised to help and yet every time he'd called from London, she had frozen him out, told him she was too busy to talk.

What could she want? His body? That tantalizing thought flirted with his mind. He'd gladly oblige, but first he'd teach her some morning-after etiquette. One does not hand one's lover his pants and usher him out the door before he's even had his coffee. "I see. Is it just me, or do you see the irony in that?"

For the first time, she had the grace to look a little discomfited. Not much, just a brief shift in her gaze, a tiny clearing of the throat. His brother, Nick, liked to boast that he had the best P.A. in the country: scarily efficient, über-professional, absolutely composed. But Adam possessed the secret to unlocking that composure. All he had to do was get close to see the way he affected her.

He stood and perched on the edge of his desk right in front of her.

"If I acted a little distant after…" she began.

He kept his brow arched and his eyes on her face. He wanted that apology. "After our unforgettable night together?"

Adam smiled when she swallowed, noting the faint tinge of pink on her cheeks.

"I apologize," she said gravely. "I'm afraid I'm not very experienced in these matters."

"Which was one of the most charming and unforgettable things about that night," Adam told her. And he meant it. For a woman in her midtwenties, she was beguilingly shy and inexperienced. "Was it not to your satisfaction?" he asked, knowing the question would discomfit her, and that she had been satisfied several times over.

Her skin pinked even more and he could tell she'd embedded her teeth into the inside of her cheek.

"I'm very sorry, Adam," she told him earnestly. "It was a special night, one I'll never forget."

Adam held her eyes for a few seconds more, then nodded. He deserved no less, but the apology seemed to be from the heart and his anger dissolved. Besides, having her grovel put the ball firmly in his court. She had come to him. He wanted what only she could give him.

And presumably, she wanted him, or else why was she here? "What can I do for you, Jasmine?" he asked, settling back on the desk to give her a modicum more breathing space. He folded his arms, intrigued now that his pride had been restored.

Jasmine swallowed again and looked him directly in the eye. "I want you to spend Christmas with me at my family's estate in Lincolnshire," she said. "As my fiancé."

In the shocking silence that followed, Jasmine forced herself to keep her eyes on his handsome face. She must stay calm and controlled, act as if this was just an everyday request and not the most preposterous thing she'd ever done in her life.

Under his short, razor-textured dark hair, his forehead creased in surprise. His toffee-colored eyes were wide with astonishment. Designer stubble and sideburns normally turned her right off but the moment she'd met Adam Thorne, playboy, high-flyer, and—according to his brother—a shameless flirt and womanizer, she was mesmerized. Model good looks, a tall, lean build that looked oh-so-good in his designer suits and trendy open-necked shirts.

Now all traces of his heart-stopping smile had vanished, his full lips pursed as he stared at her intently. Lord, why had she come out with it just like that? She should have worked up to it.

Jasmine bit her lip, cursing the long flight that seemed to have loaded her brain with cotton wool and feeling less than her best physically. For some reason, a few weeks ago, this interesting and very sexy man had found her attractive. Today, she felt as dull and dowdy as the winter's day outside.

"Perhaps I should expand a little."

She never volunteered details about her family, not to Adam, Nick or anyone. It was easier that way, to shun relationships, not get close to people. She'd fled England five years ago to get away from her colorful past.

On the morning after they'd finally slept together, Adam had asked her about a magazine article she'd cut out and left on her coffee table. At the time, Jasmine was distracted, admiring his naked chest, the long line of his spine, the length and sheer fluid beauty of his legs as he walked around her lounge.

Distracted mostly by the utter novelty of having a gorgeous naked man walking around her lounge.

"That's my uncle," she'd responded to his question before realizing the danger. Adam lived in London. He might have heard something. He might mention it to Nick. She couldn't bear it if her few New Zealand friends and colleagues found out about the complicated circumstances that had dogged her all her life.

Jasmine had panicked, barely hearing him as he told her he'd been trying to get hold of the great Stewart Cooper—the subject of the article—for two months, and maybe she could get him an introduction. "Yes, probably," she'd told him, thrusting his shirt and trousers at him, making excuses that she was late for something, sorry, have a good trip back to London, thanks for everything. She had practically closed the door on his goodbye kiss, full of regrets because it had been the best night of her life and now it was spoiled.

But she hadn't worried about it for too long. Adam Thorne was hardly likely to remember her. That was one of the reasons she'd indulged herself, that and the fact he was heading back to London in the next couple of days.

He had called, as it happened, several times. She'd managed to stay cool and vague and after a couple more calls, he stopped asking how her garden was looking, had she been dancing lately and was Nick working her too hard. He only asked about her uncle.

She'd stammered that she was too busy to talk, she hadn't been able to contact him. Jasmine felt terrible, but what could she do? She'd never met her uncle. Never wanted to because of the bad blood between him and her father. And according to her father, he'd never wanted to meet her. Really, she'd done Adam a favor. Stewart Cooper, the reclusive billionaire, might never agree to see him if he knew Jasmine was a friend.

Now, she cautioned herself against telling him more than he needed to know. "Firstly, my name isn't Jasmine. It's Jane."

Adam frowned, pursing his lips, and she nearly smiled when he softly formed the word a couple of times, *Jane,* as if testing it on his lips.

Then he shook his head. "Doesn't do it for me, sorry."

"I haven't changed it officially," she told him, digging her fat traveling wallet out of her bag. She slid her passport from its compartment, opened it and showed him. "My passport and official documents are still Jane."

"Jasmine suits you better," he insisted, glancing at the passport.

She wondered with trepidation if her next words would get a reaction. "My father is a retired barrister, Sir Nigel Cooper?" She raised her brows in query.

Adam shook his head again.

She took a breath, maintaining eye contact while relief coursed through her. He hadn't heard of her father or her. She could scarcely believe it. But then, he'd only been in London four years, arriving more than a year after the scandal that caused Jane Cooper to become almost as prominent a household name as Princess Di—and not for the first time in her life. "He and my stepmother live at Pembleton Estate. It's a two-thousand acre estate in Lincolnshire. A stately home, part of which is open to the public." Again, Adam looked nonplussed, but she wouldn't expect him to be interested in English stately homes.

Now for the difficult part. "My father needs a male heir, a son or grandson to be able to keep the estate. Since my older brother died as a toddler, Father has always been very keen to see me married."

"You mean, like an arranged marriage?" Adam asked, leaning back and crossing his legs. "Do people still do that?"

"I expect he thought I'd take care of things myself," Jasmine said dryly. "Anyway, he's recently been diagnosed with a brain tumor. I'm afraid it's very advanced." The tumor was slow-growing, but her father had apparently ignored the signs for much too long. Jasmine was haunted by the thought that if she had been here, she may have seen the signs or persuaded him to be vigilant about medical appointments.

Adam made the usual platitudes of regret.

Jasmine continued, telling him her father even had a suitor for her in mind. "Our neighbor. He's an old school friend of mine."

"The wicked prince," Adam murmured.

Jasmine smiled. "He's not. He is a nice man, but I have no intention of marrying him."

She knew this must sound strange to someone who hadn't grown up in the rarefied atmosphere of English gentry, with all the tradition and history that was still alive and well in the country estates.

Jasmine looked down at her hands. "This is going to be a rather fraught visit. It's almost certainly Father's last Christmas. I…" She exhaled, feeling childish. Get it over with, she urged herself. Who knows? Adam may find the whole thing a lark.

But it wasn't. She had been a disappointment to her father all her life. She just wanted to please him, once, and have the memory that she'd done so. "I'm afraid I told an untruth a couple of months ago. I told him I was already engaged."

"And that's where I come in." He suddenly leaned forward quickly, fixing her with an intense look. "Why me, by the way?"

*Because you are unaware of my past,* she thought. *Because I felt guilty about the way I treated you. Because I wanted to see you again…* "I don't know very many men," she said truthfully. At least, not many that didn't pity her or think she was a laughingstock.

"And when your father asks about the wedding… where we're going to live…the pitter-patter of tiny feet?"

"We'll be suitably vague," she answered with confidence. "My father and I don't see eye to eye about some things." Most things, she thought. "Our relationship is quite distant. I am close to my stepmother, Gill. She may ask questions but probably not in front of him, and she's very discreet."

Adam's eyes never left her face. Jasmine mentally crossed her fingers and toes, knowing it was a lot to ask at such short notice. He was bound to have plans. She had thought about calling but hoped a surprise attack might have better results.

Still unsmiling, his eyes assessed her. If only she could turn the clock back and play that last morning again, or the phone calls afterward. Adam used to look at her with such regard.

He hadn't lost the habit, however, of maneuvering himself too close to her. Jasmine wished he'd sit at his desk rather than on it because he was too close for comfort. He always had been.

As if he read her mind, he suddenly sat up a little straighter. "And will your uncle be present at this family Christmas?"

She had expected him to ask. And in the scheme of things, this was the most important point of all. She kept her reply crisp. "No. He and my father have had a small falling out and it would be best not to mention him." Illness or not, the whole of Lincolnshire would hear Sir Nigel's roars if anyone mentioned his nemesis's name.

She softened her voice, plumping for sympathy.

"Since this may well be his last Christmas, I'd hate to upset him."

Adam's sharp eyes searched her face. She held his gaze steadily, waiting for his reply.

"For a favor of this magnitude," he said slowly, "and considering I have plans for Christmas…"

"Do you?"

"I *always* have plans, Jasmine." Adam smiled but there was little warmth in it. "Is there any good reason I should put myself out for you when you virtually ran me out of your house a few weeks ago?"

Friends were not a commodity Jasmine was flush with, but she had enjoyed every minute of their dates, of doing things she hadn't done before, the parry and thrust of his attempts to charm her into bed. "I thought we were friends."

She reminded herself that friends don't, as a rule, have hot, sweaty, plentiful sex in nearly every room in her house. Incredibly though, the experience had left her with such good—no, great—memories, it wouldn't worry her if Adam Thorne was her last lover ever. Who else could possibly measure up?

A shiver went through her and judging by the sudden flare of attention in his eyes, he'd noticed. She swallowed quickly. He couldn't know what steamy recollections had just filled her mind. Or how, all of a sudden, she could identify mint and orange blossom in his cologne. Or was so attuned to his breathing, her own emulated it. Nor how bloody attractive she found the way his fierce brows feathered a little on either side of the bridge of his nose.

"Friends help each other out," he murmured.

She closed her eyes and began to despair. Adam used the same voice as he had the night he finally persuaded her that she wanted him as much as he did her. Why deny each other, he'd said, when sex was such a natural and pleasurable way to show appreciation? That voice was her downfall; sultry, suggestive and warm, it coated the senses like honey on ham. Erotic images of their night together, his whispers inciting her to do things she'd never dreamed she could do, had her toes curling in latent pleasure.

For the first time—unless in her overheated state, she was imagining it—his eyes warmed a little—a lot. Adam Thorne knew exactly what she was thinking.

"Oh, I'm not discounting *that,* lovely Jasmine," he confirmed a second later, his deep, soft voice raising the hairs on the back of her neck. "Believe me, I remember every spectacular, soft, passionate inch of you."

She sucked in a breath to try to contain a pulse gone mad. Heat bloomed on her cheeks and all the way down her body. How did he do it, send her senses wild without even a touch? He used to toy with her at work, sitting on her desk, talking of nothing very much in that velvety voice of his, watching her with eyes that would tempt a saint. She'd thought it was about needling his brother or shattering her good-girl reputation. His effect on her was powerful and he knew it.

"That's not on the agenda this trip," she said, not as firmly as she would have liked. Which of them was she trying to convince?

She had to shoot him down. There were more important priorities than her own selfish desires. "I slept with you in a moment of weakness, not expecting to see you again. I wasn't looking for anything more."

Adam chuckled. "Well, I'm certainly not in the market for a relationship. But back to your 'agenda—'" he held up his index finger to indicate quote marks "—there doesn't seem to be an equitable balance of mutual reward between friends here."

Jasmine's desire seeped away. She knew what he wanted, but if he discovered the full extent of the hatred between her father and uncle, she would cease to be of use to him. She had to gloss over the family feud, at least until he was there at the estate, accepting their hospitality. Hopefully his good manners and charm would do the rest.

"All I want," Adam prompted, "is the introduction. The rest is up to me."

Seeing the determination on his face, Jasmine realized glossing over it wouldn't be enough. This man preferred something a little more concrete.

With six months to a year left to live, her father's happiness was her first priority. With no idea how she would go about it, Jasmine summoned up a self-assurance she didn't feel. "If you do this for me, I

give you my word I will set it up—" She hesitated
and then said firmly, "—after Christmas."

"Good." Adam got up and went back to his side
of the desk. "Now that's settled, there is one more
thing…"

Jasmine was already half way to her feet, prepar-
ing to depart.

"It's the annual company Christmas bash tonight.
I've been too busy to find a date. Come with me."

Even as she reluctantly agreed, Jasmine had a
sinking feeling about this. The more time she spent
in Adam Thorne's company, the more she wanted to
spend. Hopefully her good intentions wouldn't get
her into trouble.

Then again, she'd had few enough opportunities
to feel like a woman over the last few years.

Adam Thorne made her feel all woman.

# Two

Adam picked her up in a silver Mercedes cabriolet that smelled brand-new, and took her to a trendy club only a short drive from her hotel.

"What name are we going by tonight?" he asked as they waited to be checked off the guest list.

"Just Jasmine," she said firmly, and it suddenly occurred to her she may be recognized. This was the kind of place some of her friends from five years ago might have frequented. She looked around warily, hoping that her long dark hair was different enough from the shaggy, lighter style she went with back then.

They made their way to a mezzanine, where about a hundred VIP guests of Croft, Croft and Bayley milled about. Almost immediately, well-wishers swamped them and she learned that tonight doubled as the annual corporate Christmas function, as well as Adam's farewell from the company. She looked around in amazement at the incredible interior. Every wall depicted what appeared to be a blue waterfall of vertical lines of numbers.

"Very high-tech, isn't it?" Adam smiled at her open-mouthed wonder. "Corporate clients can digitally design their own colors and atmosphere—or their brand, if they want to be boring—onto computers and have that imagery projected onto the walls for their event." He explained that Croft, Croft and Bayley had gone for a stock-exchange depiction tonight, but he'd been here when heaving blue seas seemed to crash against the walls. He'd seen panoramic landscapes of canyons that almost echoed, and meadows filled with nodding wildflowers in a gentle breeze. "You could come here every night of the week and feel you're somewhere different." He shook his head. "I liked the idea so much, I bought into it."

"You own this club?"

Adam shook his head. "Just a percentage of the multimedia company that came up with the concept."

Jasmine knew that innovative and daring ideas intrigued Adam. That was the catalyst for his start-up business, to give talented people with big ideas the means and expertise to go global.

She accepted a glass of champagne from a Santahatted waitress and was introduced to too many people to count. While Adam chatted, one of the senior partners extolled her escort's virtues. "I first saw him on the floor of the exchange four years ago, making money hand over fist as a day trader. A successful trader should be passionate about markets, rather than trading. While everyone else ran around in a panic, Adam just sat there, watching, sticking to his plan. I knew we had to have him."

As the night progressed, she heard much more of Adam's ambition, how hard he'd worked to attain his high level of success.

"The youngest-ever partner in this company," another partner confided. Croft, Croft and Bayley wasn't the biggest stockbrokerage in the city, but it was one of the oldest and most venerated. "We'll miss him but we're too small to contain his ambition." Another of his colleagues told her that the new business was risky but if anyone could pull it off, Adam could.

All this left Jasmine a little confused and a lot impressed. Until today, her preconception of Adam Thorne, based on their half-dozen outings in New Zealand, had been of a fun-loving, sexy and rich young man, an opinion reinforced by his brother's declaration that he wasn't to be taken seriously. Nick loved his brother, she knew that, but looking around at the army of admirers, the breathtaking backdrop of moving numbers, the copious bottles of French champagne and decadent hors d'oeuvres, she couldn't help feeling Nick hadn't given enough credit to Adam's work ethic.

The formalities of the evening commenced as the partners wished their staff a happy Christmas and then made a special presentation to bid Adam farewell and wish him good luck for what was sure to be a stellar future. Jasmine watched the proceedings from well back in the crowd, feeling sorry for every other man in the place. It was unfair that one man should be so overendowed, not only with good looks and vitality, but success, too. Not so long ago, she'd thought Nick Thorne the most handsome man she knew. He was bigger than Adam but similar enough in coloring, athleticism and those hypnotic eyes, so she'd been as surprised as anyone when it came out recently that Nick was adopted.

But they were as different as night and day. Nick was straight-A all the way, a brilliant but conservative businessman in his expensive suits and neatly cropped hair. Jasmine tried and failed to imagine him tossing an old rugby ball around his office, or even with his feet up on the desk. Never in a million years.

Adam Thorne probably didn't even know how to knot a tie. Certainly she'd never seen him in one, not even the night last month he'd escorted her to the Royal New Zealand Ballet. Style oozed devilishly from every pore. His fierce brows and the stubble shadowing his jawline and full sexy lips lent him a bad-boy demeanor, even though his smile was a lot more ready than Nick's.

While she'd been busy daydreaming, another half hour had passed and the formalities wound up. Adam returned from the front of the room and drew her into his side.

"Very nice," he said in that low, sultry voice, leaning so close his lips almost touched her earlobe.

Jasmine shivered, knowing that he felt it since he'd placed one hand lightly on the small of her back. If that hadn't alerted her, his self-satisfied smile when he drew back did.

"What?" she asked casually. Adam Thorne was too discerning for his own good.

"Being the object of your avid attention."

So she'd been staring. "I believe it's polite, when listening to a speech, to pay attention to the speaker."

Adam's grin only widened. "You can be very *English* sometimes, Ms. Cooper."

He was playing with her. He knew the effect he had on her and was using her gratitude to his full advantage. But Jasmine had her pride and after all, he wanted something from her, too.

Aside from sex…she resisted the urge to fan her hot face and thought it best to change the tone of the conversation. "I think Nick would have been very proud of you tonight."

His surprise at her comment showed in the slight arch of one dark brow. Jasmine wasn't sure if it was the subject matter or just the change of direction but when he pursed his lips a second later, she saw that he was pleased. And that, funnily enough, pleased her.

"You'll never guess!" A young colleague of Adam's joined their small group, brimming with a sly kind of excitement that Jasmine recognized as typical of a gossip. "Which esteemed royal is in the gents', popping party pills right this minute?"

"Vincent de Burgh," someone said quickly.

"Not again!" Another member of their party rolled his eyes.

Jasmine's heart plummeted and she almost swayed on her feet. Vincent de Burgh, notorious playboy, tenth in line to the British throne, and the man whose betrayal five years ago sent her packing to the other side of the world.

Careful not to turn her head, she looked for the bathrooms, which she located on the first level. She then scrutinized the messenger's face, wondering if he was telling her in a roundabout way that he knew she had once been engaged to the very same royal louse fittingly off his face in a toilet.

The young executives compared recent stories about the troublesome royal, not giving her any particular interest. Satisfied it was just idle celebrity gossip, Jasmine relaxed slightly. Nonetheless, she couldn't afford to stay here and risk being recognized.

That Vincent was still behaving badly didn't surprise her. She'd heard he recently divorced the

woman he ditched her for—her ex-best friend—and
no doubt was drowning his sorrows and searching for
some other rich, deluded female. The unfathomable
thing was that he always succeeded, as her father had
repeatedly warned her.

She turned to Adam, her mind racing. If he found
out about her high-profile engagement, it would take
just one Google hit to find out the rest. All she needed
was tomorrow, one day, to play happy couples at the
estate. Then Adam could leave "on business" and she
could continue her holiday and spend some quality
time with her father before she had to get back to
work. She didn't expect to have to keep the pretense
up for too long. Her father was getting weaker and
more forgetful by the day, according to Gill. In two
or three months, he might not comprehend anything,
and if he did, then she would tell him that sadly, she
and Adam hadn't worked out.

But if Adam discovered before tomorrow how ac-
rimonious the relations were between her father and
Stewart, she could kiss her Christmas Day goodwill
mission goodbye.

Adam's eyes were on her face and she realized
she'd been staring again. He had his back to the con-
veniences on the ground floor and she flicked a
glance to the door of the men's toilets, just in time to
see an older, but by the look of him, most un-wiser,
Vincent lurch out.

Jasmine froze. He seemed to be looking directly up

at her but it was hard to tell with the lighting in here. After a moment, he turned toward the bar, stripping off his jacket as he did. While breathing out relief, she relished the rather nasty thought that her ex had not weathered the passing of years well. Too much good living showed in his paunch and the way his thick neck battled to be reined in by his tie. It may have been the lighting but his previously thick, sandy hair looked wispy from her vantage point on the mezzanine.

She watched as he joined a small group of men at the bar. The private function on the mezzanine had waiter service so he was obviously not part of the Croft, Croft and Bayley group. Jasmine began to breathe again.

Adam touched her arm and she brought her eyes back to his face.

"I'd like you to meet someone."

She shook hands with John Hadlow, Adam's new business partner, and his wife, Sherrilyn.

"I see why you've stood us up for Christmas, old boy," John said jovially.

Jasmine bit back a smile and glanced at Adam's face. Had he deliberately given her the impression his plans were more romantic than Christmas dinner with this pleasant couple? She apologized for upsetting everyone's schedule.

Half an hour later, she had almost forgotten about Vincent when a break in the music exposed an altercation by the stairs. She glanced over to see her ex-fiancé arguing loudly with a security man, who blocked his entrance into the private function. She spun around quickly, looking for Adam and hearing Vincent's voice clearly over the myriad conversations surrounding her. "Do you know who I am?"

Adam was a couple of feet away, talking to an attractive blonde. What to do? She could hole up in the ladies', or just pray the security guard remained aloof about Vincent's lineage. There were two stairways on either side of the mezzanine leading down. Jasmine contemplated making a dash for it down the left-hand side while Vincent was engaged with the bouncer on the right.

Her heart pounded in near panic. If he accosted her, she could claim not to know him—or she could just come clean and tell Adam the truth; that she was persona non grata to her uncle and didn't have the tiniest chance of setting up a meeting between them.

"But I just want to say a quick hallo to someone," Vincent insisted loudly to the staunch security man.

Making a decision, and hoping she wouldn't live to regret it, Jasmine walked up to stand beside Adam and slid her arm around his waist, inside his jacket. Sucked in a breath against the impact of lean, muscled torso, a very appealing male cologne and the peculiar pheromones or hormones that always had her off-kilter with this particular man. Absorbing the jolt to her senses, she bravely waited as he slowly turned his head to her. Yes, cool blonde or not, she had his full attention.

"Sorry," she said apologetically to his companion. Lifting up on tiptoe, and without removing her hand from his body, she put her lips directly onto his ear. "I think the jet lag has just caught up with me," she whispered, ensuring her lips caressed his ear with each syllable.

Adam had bowed his head in deference to his greater height. Now he turned his face and looked down into hers. His eyes burned gold, interest and wariness flickering.

Jasmine reached up toward his ear again but because he had turned his head, her cheek brushed his, thrilling her with the contact. "That," she whispered seductively, "or the champagne."

He moved as she withdrew, so that his cheek blocked hers from retreat. Triumph, query and a wolfish sort of warning blazed out from the golden depths of his eyes. If there wasn't so much at stake, she would have run to save herself. The message was clear: *Don't play with me.* Or maybe that was just her guilty conscience.

After a second's hesitation, he became all concern and solitude, making his excuses to the blonde, saying goodbye to John, shaking hands with people as they prepared to go.

And moving toward the wrong staircase. Vincent was still there, of course. She'd learned during their engagement that when he didn't get his own way, the arguments lasted for days.

"This way." She tugged on his arm, nodding at the other staircase. "I need to visit the ladies'."

They veered to the right. "You don't have to come," she told him rather half-heartedly once they were at the bottom of the stairs, glancing around fearfully in case His Royal Highness emerged from the sea of people celebrating Christmas Eve. "It's your big night, I feel guilty."

She did feel guilty about spoiling his big night, but not too guilty. And she would prefer he didn't hang around without her in case Vincent bailed him up and asked about her.

No sign of him, though, and no sign that Adam was disposed to let her disappear into the night. There was a nasty moment on the way to the exit when a photographer came from nowhere, his camera up. "The man of the hour. Quick photo for the *Out and About* magazine?"

Luckily Jasmine was able to melt judiciously into the ladies' directly beside her, hoping it would not seem ungracious.

Nothing eventuated and soon they were at Adam's car. "Feeling better?" he asked as she strapped herself in. He started the car but made no effort to put it into gear.

"Much." She allowed herself to relax a little. It was a close call but the ends justified the means and now they were safe. "I'm sorry about this. I could just take a cab…"

Adam reached over and picked up her hand. "What sort of fiancé would I be if I didn't look after you?"

He lifted her hand to his mouth and pressed his lips to the pulse point on her wrist. Her bones melted as he nibbled and sucked at the sensitive point. Suddenly, Jasmine was in real danger of keeling over and it had nothing to do with jet lag. A warm flush bathed her as she imagined a thousand arrows of fire wove a prickly scarf on the back of her neck. Her skin felt tight and stretched, her insides jumped about nervously while her mouth was as arid as the desert. "Wha-what are you doing?" she asked.

The big motor purred. Adam didn't answer right away, engrossed in driving her mad with equal parts delight and trepidation. Then he lowered her hand and spoke with the honeyed, seductive tone he'd used before. "Let's just say I'm getting into character for tomorrow." He brought her hand to his mouth again, kissing each fingertip.

Just for a moment more she wanted to enjoy this, the desire that raced through her veins, her heart beating a tattoo on her rib cage. Maybe it was jet lag, because Jasmine was a sensible woman. Why else would she seriously consider succumbing to the incredible pull to move closer, drink in the heat coming off him in waves of male scented sensuality? It wasn't right that this man should have such a monopoly on her innermost desires and be able to exploit them at will.

Summoning every ounce of concentration and willpower, Jasmine stiffened her fingers and tugged until he let go. For good measure, she turned her face to the front, knowing that his strong-boned face, those wicked lips branding her flesh, turned her on unbearably. She'd never missed sex until she'd tasted it with him.

Adam's laugh was almost inaudible in the hum of the car, but decadently amused. "I enjoy watching you squirm, Jasmine, if only because it's out of character."

She huffed out a breath, her cheeks burning. "I don't know what you mean."

She didn't look at him again until they'd pulled up outside her hotel. The moment the car stopped, she released the seat belt and opened the door, welcoming the freezing blast of air on her hot face.

Adam's eyes were still amused. "About nine?"

Jasmine nodded and closed the door.

A couple of minutes later, she swept back the curtains in her deluxe room, sank down onto a chair and looked out over Trafalgar Square and the world's most famous Christmas tree. Her stepmother, Gill, had first brought her to see the tree when she was only six or seven and she'd been many times since. Strings of vertical lights draped the huge Norwegian spruce, picking out the snowflakes as they fell. It was a magical sight, one that should have felt familiar and soothing.

She wasn't soothed. Her nerves felt chafed raw.

In the last five years she thought she'd found peace, if not happiness. From the way Adam had been talking, it wouldn't be long before he was back in New Zealand, probably Wellington, laughing and teasing and driving her mad with lust. Why had she slept with him? Far from satisfying her sexual curiosity, it had only served to make her want him more.

# Three

The drive from London took longer than expected because of a thick snow flurry, but finally they arrived at the estate just in time for lunch. Jasmine's apprehension and excitement built as they passed through the heavy wrought-iron gates. She loved the drive up to the house. Fallow deer grazed in the wooded parkland. She pointed out the stud farm her father established a decade ago. Snow dusted the reeds around the lake fronting the house.

Pembleton, originally a large Georgian house, had been greatly added to in the years before the First World War and now lent itself more to the Edwardian era.

Even Adam expressed his admiration as they slowly approached the great dun-colored house, whose dimensions more resembled a terraced street than one residence. Jasmine sighed with pride. She might have grown up here and certainly had her share of bad memories of the place, but the house and setting still took her breath away.

"How many rooms?" Adam asked as they pulled up in front of the massive porticoed entrance.

"Over a hundred, though half of it is closed up."

Her stepmother, Gill, burst out of the door and raced down the steps. Sixty years young, a petite, iron-gray-haired bundle of energy and efficiency, she greeted them with a volley of warm squeals.

"Your father is having a good day," she told them, "and is quite excited about meeting Adam, even if he probably won't show it."

Jasmine didn't take offense that her father was more excited about meeting Adam than seeing his daughter. She had always been a disappointment to him, first by being born a girl, and then when she became the willful teenager who defied his wishes.

But in his distant manner, Sir Nigel did seem pleased to see her. He sat in his comfortable chair by the fireplace and inspected her for a minute or more while clasping one of her hands with both of his. Jasmine—Jane, to them—tried to conceal her shock at his frail appearance. He'd always been a burly man—that's where she got her height from, since her mother had apparently been tiny. His most notable feature had always been his booming voice but there was little evidence of it today, except occasionally when addressing Adam. He was a shadow of his former self.

Jasmine grappled with guilt. She should be here to take care of him instead of leaving everything to Gill. She'd been with the family since Jasmine was ten years old. Gill was the warmest thing about her childhood and beyond.

They ate Christmas lunch in the formal dining room, a room that had, in the past, hosted banquets for heads of state. Among many great portraits on the walls there was a Madonna and child painted by Murillo hanging over the antique fireplace. They sat at one end of the massive table for "One's table should never exceed the nine muses," Gill liked to say.

As usual there was a daunting array of food—quail; turkey, roast beef; a whole salmon, pink and delicious; vegetables of every variety and then Christmas steamed pudding and brandy sauce with Gill's folly, ancient threepences hidden within. Jasmine had pre-warned Adam of this eccentricity to avoid breaking a tooth.

Afterward, her father insisted Gill take the seal off an old bottle of port and they adjourned to the more informal drawing room.

"So you're engaged at last," her father said croakily,

settling into his chair. Adam and Jasmine sat on an overstuffed antique couch opposite her father while Gill served the drinks.

This would be the awkward part but she didn't expect there would be many questions. Her father would not care who she married, as long as his estate was looked after. "Yes, we are," she replied, trying to sound excited.

"When is the wedding? Will it be here?"

Adam's arm slipped around her shoulder and she tried not to flinch. "As soon as possible," he murmured, "as far as I'm concerned."

Jasmine's smile didn't slip but every muscle in her body tensed up and her mind raced. "We haven't had time to discuss it," she said, before burying her nose in her port.

Her father's head raised. "Well, six months, a year?"

Her heart went out to him. With a death sentence hanging over his head, of course he wanted a date to grasp on to. "We'll discuss it while we're on holiday and let you know."

"Hmph." Her father subsided back into the seat, picking at the rug Gill had put over his knees. "I'll have to announce it."

"No!"

Jasmine's sharp response had all eyes swiveling to her face. She swallowed down the panic that comment had instigated. "I'd really prefer to keep this just within the family, if possible."

Her father gave her a spiteful look. "My daughter, the procrastinator," he muttered.

She heard Adam's quick indrawn breath and couldn't look at him.

"That's understandable, dear," Gill said sympathetically.

Adam's hand slid around and surreptitiously tugged on her ponytail. "I'm all for shouting it from the rooftops," he said in a low voice that only she could hear.

Jasmine resisted the shiver of awareness that generated and kept her eyes on her father, amazed he would even suggest a public announcement after what happened with Vincent nearly six years ago. When the story broke that her fiancé and her best friend had run off into the sunset together just a month before her wedding, she hadn't been able to leave the house without paparazzi on her tail. That was when she realized she could never escape her past. All her hopes and dreams crashed in spectacular style, played out in the media, and she decided to move as far away as she could get. Somewhere where no one knew of her infamous past, and hopefully never would.

"Have you spoken to Ian recently?" her father asked, his stern gaze losing none of its sharpness despite the ravages of age and illness.

"No." Jasmine sighed. "Should I have?"

"Who's Ian?" Adam leaned forward to set his port

glass down. His brows were raised and his knee pressed against hers.

She gave him a cool glance. If you asked her, he was playing the amorous fiancé just a little too well for her liking. "A friend. Our neighbor." She had told him about Ian—the little she wanted him to know at this point.

"A little more than a friend I think," her father murmured.

Ian had been there all her life. They were the same age, had played together as children. He was her friend—until her father decided he would make an ideal husband. "He's steady, a hard worker, and boys run in that family," he declared. "Plus he will inherit the adjoining thousand acres. That gives us options to expand the estate and generate more income."

From the time she was eighteen, her father never let up but Jasmine gave no serious consideration to a union. When her past and present collided with vivid impact, Ian was there to pick up the pieces. Because he was the only one in the world who didn't look at her as if she had two heads, and because her father did all in his power to push them together, she went out with him for a couple of months and tried to think of him as more than a friend. She even slept with him, but there was no chemistry there for her.

They usually got together for a coffee or a meal on her annual trips home but she hadn't felt obliged to let him know she was coming. Besides, she knew he was in Switzerland for Christmas.

Now everyone, Adam included, was looking at her as if she was a jezebel. "He's a friend," she repeated firmly, sipping her port.

"Hmph." Her father glared at her hands. "No ring?"

"We plan to remedy that on this visit, don't we, darling?" Adam took her free hand and squeezed it. "Antwerp or Amsterdam?"

Jasmine smiled faintly and forced herself to relax her fingers, one by one, while thinking of ways to kill him.

Thankfully the excitement and port had worn her father out and he retired shortly afterward for a nap. The blazing fire and overstuffed bellies had everyone yawning. Gill rose, saying she had made up Jasmine's room. "You are staying? And for the party tomorrow?"

Jasmine prepared to say that she would stay but not Adam, and then Gill's words filtered into her brain, setting up a wave of temptation to batter her defenses. *Her* room, she'd said. Not two rooms...

Her room where she'd played with dolls, swooned over the Backstreet Boys, experimented with clothes and makeup, fantasized over real boys, sneaked Vincent into...and then howled her anguish into her pillow when he broke her heart. What was a girl's bedroom but a catalogue of the most intimate experiences of one's life?

It couldn't get any more intimate than having Adam Thorne in her room, in amongst her personal things. Heat that had little to do with the fire and more to do with that *blasted* man caressing her fingers spread through her, dampening her forehead.

And then there was the annual Boxing Day party tomorrow that the estate put on for the locals in the district. An afternoon tea and free tour for the villagers and later, cocktails and a dinner party for closer friends and the village dignitaries. The chances of getting through the whole thing without Adam discovering the depth of hatred between her father and his brother were slim. The locals loved to gossip about the inhabitants of the estate. The family feud and her personal shame were bound to arise at some point.

"Sorry," she managed at last. "I can, but Adam has some business in town."

Her "fiancé" lifted her hand to his mouth and pressed his lips to her palm. "Nonsense. It's Christmas. We'd love to stay."

Oh, she really would have to kill him. Refusing to look at him, she gave Gill a rather strained smile and shrug.

Adam was clearly trying to embarrass and discomfit her. She set her mouth. It wouldn't work. Pembleton wasn't short on bedrooms and Jasmine knew where the bedding was kept.

Gill gave her a curious glance. Her stepmother was pretty intuitive. What was Adam playing at? She'd have thought he'd be pleased to get away from the ancient old house and her overbearing father. This just didn't seem his scene.

"I think I'll show Adam part of the house," she said, rising. "And walk off some of that wonderful dinner."

Gill nodded. "If you get hungry later, there are plenty of leftovers in the kitchen. Just help your-selves. Your father usually has his tea in his room but he might come down later."

As soon as she'd gone, Jasmine turned back to Adam and kept her voice low. "Did you have to say you'd stay?"

He remained seated, looking up at her thought-fully. "I've never stayed in a stately home before… tell me about Ian."

She missed a beat. "What about him?"

"Have you slept together?"

Jasmine pressed her lips together to stop the hot retort that sprang to mind. Something in the way his sharp gaze focused so intently on her stopped her. After a long pause, she nodded.

"I see."

What did he see? That she'd slept with him, there-fore she was obliged to marry him? A smile nearly slipped out when she thought of the dent that would put in Adam Thorne's womanizing ways.

Yet she felt compelled to justify herself. "It was comfort sex. And my father has his own acquisitive reasons for wanting me to marry Ian."

"Do I need to dust off my dueling swords?"

She let another heartbeat go by, squashing down, as she often did, all the clever things she'd wish she'd said later, when she was alone. "Would you like to see the house or not?"

Adam got up, looming tall over her. She turned toward the door but he caught her arm and turned her back. "Why did you need his comfort?"

Jasmine blinked, needing to think. Overfull, overheated, overwhelmed by him…how much did he deserve to know? She couldn't bear it if all the salacious stories got back to his brother and her colleagues. Of course she missed home, this house mostly, Gill, and sometimes her cantankerous father. But New Zealand was her haven. Her comfortable art deco house in the eastern suburbs was a far cry from the luxury and tradition of Pembleton, but she felt safe there. With one careless word, Adam could whip that safety net out from under her.

From the determined gleam in his eye, she deduced the lesser of two evils would be her failed love affair, the incident that sparked the return of all the unwelcome publicity from years before. The most important thing was to keep the feud from him, for now at least.

Jasmine looked pointedly at his hand on her arm. "A broken heart, reasonably common when you're twenty."

Adam merely raised his brows.

She sighed. "Against my father's wishes, I fell in love with the man who is tenth in line for the throne. It didn't last. He preferred my best friend. They recently divorced, but the point is, for a few months, I was a lamb to the slaughter for the press. An engagement announcement—" she gave him a scathing look "—for our *pretend* engagement might bring it all up again."

Adam's face cleared. "Vincent de Burgh. That's why you were in such a hurry to leave last night—and you didn't want your photo taken."

Jasmine nodded, not realizing he'd picked up on that.

His eyes searched her face for so long she began to fidget. Finally he nodded. "Okay. That wasn't so hard, was it?"

"What?"

"To bring me up to speed. I'm beginning to think there are more secrets hoarded up in that lovely head—" he tapped her temple with his index finger "—than currently floating around the Secret service."

Adam was enjoying himself. Despite Jasmine's stuffy father, who seemed to regard her achievements and wishes as an afterthought, her stepmother was great and the house was out of this world.

The best part was making her squirm, because as he'd pointed out last night, she didn't like it one bit. Playing her fiancé gave him carte blanche to touch, to be suggestive, to tease. He almost forgot why he was here. Oh, he wanted Jasmine—or Jane, as he had to keep reminding himself—more with each passing minute but his main goal was the opportunity to meet her uncle.

The touching, being suggestive and teasing just made it all the more enjoyable—for him.

The private apartments were bright and light, showcasing plenty of marble, plasterwork, windows and gilded furnishings. It was a different story "below stairs", as the basement was known. This is where the twenty or so servants in the early nineteen-hundreds had worked, Jasmine explained. "And that doesn't count the gardeners, farmhands, garage or stable hands. Or, would you believe, the night watchmen."

History wasn't his thing, but as they slowly wandered the areas open to the public, Adam was transported back to another time. She astounded him with her knowledge. It seemed she had a story about every nook and cranny, every priceless heirloom, every brick in the house! It was all so fascinating.

"The hall of summons," she announced, pointing out the labels where forty bells hung high on faded plaster walls, some sporting the names of some of her ancestors. She showed him the cavernous kitchen, with its incredibly high ceiling, "to dissipate the heat and steam from the coal-powered range, which could eat up to a hundredweight of coal in a day."

"How do you know all this stuff?" he marveled, declining her invitation to walk up the ninety stone stairs to the maids' quarters in the attic.

"I grew up here." She ran her hand over some ancient books in the butler's rooms—*Burke's Peerage, Baronetage and Knightage* was one tome that caught Adam's eye. "And I have a degree in English history."

He straightened, surprised. "You do?"

"Uh-huh. I got interested in history when we started a family tree at school," she explained. "It took me years to finish, even though our family has only been here for a couple of hundred years." They walked up the basement stairs into the entranceway, blinking at the strong light after the gloominess below. "I enjoyed it so much, I decided I wanted to work in a museum one day."

"And yet now you reside in one of the youngest countries in the world and work as a personal assistant in a financial organization."

Jasmine laughed. "Ironic, isn't it? Maybe Te Papa would have me."

She referred to New Zealand's national museum in Wellington. Adam's interest in Jasmine doubled. She was well-educated, cultured, elegant. She oozed class, spades of it—and it wasn't something she'd learned. Rather, she was born to it, to this grand house with hundreds of years under its belt.

As she uncovered history for him, he so wanted to uncover her many layers, to know her secrets and desires and fears and dreams. Despite her culture and poise and obvious smarts, she was vulnerable, softer than the socialites or corporate sharks he normally dated.

But Adam had a feeling unraveling Jasmine's mysteries would take a lifetime.

"Don't you miss it here, all the history, the house and the countryside?"

"Sometimes."

"Will you stay in New Zealand?" he asked.

"For now," she said pensively, neither her tone nor the brief reply a confirmation.

"What do you like about it?"

She thought for a moment. "The laid-back, fair-dues character of it. The small population. A lot of things. It just seems a more open and fair society."

Adam nodded. He missed his country often—when he wasn't working fifteen-hour days or squiring some gorgeous woman around London—and was looking forward to returning, probably within the next year, and showing his brother and father that he'd risen to the top.

They'd eat his dust. So he was an irresponsible lightweight who could not sustain his incredible success. He'd show them and raise them some. And when he'd set up in Australia and expanded into the States, perhaps by the time he was forty, he'd choose a mate and start a family. And his family would come first. Adam would not emulate his parents, who had worked six days a week for most of his childhood.

Not that he was complaining. He liked his particu-

lar set of familial individuals. He'd just come out of
the womb always wanting to do better…at everything. What was wrong with that?

That night, they said their good-nights to Gill and
he followed Jasmine up the incredible silver stairway,
which apparently took three men three days to polish
in its day. They hadn't discussed sleeping arrangements but she wasn't at ease. The stiffness of her
back as she showed him the way corroborated that.
After several fruitless dates in New Zealand, he was
conversant with her resolve.

His desire for her had only increased since their
passionate encounter last month. Far from slaking his
thirst, he was parched to the bone. She'd been very
proper throughout the day, even when he pushed the
boundaries a little, touching her, whispering in her
ear, all the little nuances that hopefully had her father
and stepmother believing they were a couple.

She hadn't cracked. He admired her composure
but it only made him more determined to break it. He
thought back to some of the dark rooms "below
stairs" and imagined there was a ghost or two clank-
ing around this mausoleum—perhaps he could play
the "afraid of the dark card"…

She opened a door and showed him into a bedroom that would fit most of his town house inside.
The room and salon were tastefully decorated in
sage green, overlooking an Italian fountain in the lily
pond, and with the ubiquitous fire crackling in the

antique fireplace. This house must be hellish cold, he thought, with the number of fireplaces throughout.

"Don't tell me this was your actual room?" He touched the four-poster bed that looked the size of an Olympic swimming pool. He was amazed anyone could sleep here. The furniture and decor belonged in a palace.

"Mmm." She walked over to their bags, which the housekeeper had brought up from the entrance. Watching her, it suddenly hit Adam that she'd grown up here, this was a slice of her life, with all its pomp and ceremony and tradition.

And yet it just didn't mesh with the shy woman he knew in Wellington. Her home was comfortable, small, with a bright garden full of camellias and rhododendrons, but not luxurious by any means.

Adam blew out a long breath, it suddenly occurring to him that Jasmine was serious money. Not that he cared about having money half as much as the making of it. But with her obvious love of history, her family so ancient and well-connected, how could she turn her back on this and expect to find happiness in a country where only the odd tree dated back more than a couple of centuries?

She belonged here, couldn't she see that?

Jasmine picked up her bag and headed for the door. Adam leaned on the fireplace, knowing she was too well-mannered to leave without saying good-night.

She turned at the door, gifting him a small smile. "Sleep well."

"That's a fine way to say good-night to your fiancé," he said in a low, teasing voice.

She shifted the overnight bag into her other hand. Her eyes were wary but not hostile. "You're enjoying this, I believe."

Adam's head went up, his smile ready. He always enjoyed the chase. She should know that! "I am, I admit it."

And he wasn't just teasing. He enjoyed seeing her in her natural environment. "It's like a different world."

"Good night, Adam," she said quietly, looking into his face, and as always happened when they looked at each other, the overpowering attraction leaped to life between them, boosting his anticipation.

Then she blinked rapidly and began to back away toward the door. Adam spoke quickly. "And now you're going to leave me to the mercy of the resident ghosts and go off to some crypt somewhere, because you don't trust yourself in the same room with me."

Yes, he was disappointed. The desire he felt for her was much too intense for a woman he had already slept with. What was this hold she had over him?

Jasmine smiled gently. "The ghosts are friendly and I'll pass on the crypt, but I should be safe in the maids' quarters in the attic."

Adam nodded. "Ninety stairs should render you relatively safe, yes."

Again she turned to go, then stopped. "Thank you for this."

Simply said, classy. He *really* liked this woman—but he had to remember what his purpose here was. His whole life stretched out in front of him, time enough for distractions. But for now, he had a new business to contend with, people who depended on him.

He shrugged carelessly. "You want something. I want something."

Often he'd thought Jasmine's eyes looked sad. If not sad, then as if they were expecting something to make them sad in the very near future. Now she stood in the doorway, both hands grasping the strap on her holdall, her chin tucked into her chest, and her eyes almost silver in the firelight, filled with sadness and secrets.

"Of course," she said, and left the room.

# Four

A weak sun came out on Boxing Day, so Jasmine decided to show Adam the grounds of the estate. They took her father's four-wheel drive and motored slowly around the two-thousand acres. There were a couple of hundred acres of woodland and grazing for fallow deer, the thoroughbred stud, stables and track and expansive but basically disused parklands, backed by rocky, heather-covered hills behind the house.

"Father always said he'd like to develop a golf course here. I don't know why he hasn't."

"How many staff look after all this?" Adam asked. She told him that the estate retained only a small staff of a live-in housekeeper, part-time cleaners and kitchen hands, cook, tour guide and gardener. "Plus the stud manager," Jasmine finished. "It's not nearly enough. We need an agricultural specialist, first and foremost. Gill still handles most of the administrative tasks, but she hasn't kept up with learning new techniques and technology." She turned her face to the house in the distance. "And I doubt she'll have time for the next few months."

Jasmine had many ideas for improving the estate, although her personal choice would be to concentrate on the house and heirlooms first.

"All those empty rooms could be put to such good use," she mused, her mind clicking into second gear. "An antiques center, private exhibitions, niche weekends for small groups like writers and such, small conferences, weddings…" There were endless possibilities that excited her but not, sadly, her more conservative father. "Father doesn't hold with the modern trend of opening up stately homes to the public. He's had to, to some extent, to keep up with the maintenance costs, but it's a struggle getting him to listen to any new ideas."

"With you in charge," Adam commented, "Pembleton could be a world-class venue."

She smiled at him and gazed around at the snow-dusted landscape. Perhaps absence did make the heart fonder. Or the reality of her father's mortality brought it all closer to home. She had loved the house and the land, would always love it, but the memories that remained at the edges of her mind were of distance, of being let down. She'd always been convinced that the events in her early life colored how her father saw her, ultimately as a burden and a disappointment. She had long accepted that they would never be close, and that that wasn't her fault. But after Vincent, the place became a prison. And if she'd gone along with her father's wishes to marry Ian, it would be her prison now.

They drove into the village and stopped for a pint at the local pub. She acknowledged the curious stares of the locals, a few of whom she remembered vaguely. Suddenly she was glad she lived in New Zealand. Just something so small as to be able to drink a coffee or a beer in public, without everyone speculating on your love life or your parents' tragedy of a marriage, was worth the pangs of regret she sometimes suffered when thinking about home.

"Is that little Jane Cooper?" the barmaid asked.

Jasmine trawled her memory banks. "How are you, Mrs. Dainty?"

They chatted for a minute or two about the sad state of her father's health. "Some families have their share of tragedy," the pleasant woman said, shaking her head, "but yours has had more than most."

"What did she mean?" Adam asked as they took a table by the fireplace.

Jasmine had spent a good part of the night, bedded down in a room four doors away from Adam, thinking about him. Wishing that she could separate sex from emotion, because her emotions were going haywire with him around.

She didn't regret that she'd slept with him a few weeks ago, but involving him in her family affairs could turn out to be the biggest regret of all, because despite his arrogance and his teasing, he was dangerously likeable.

She looked at him over the rim of her beer, felt the kick in the pit of her stomach whenever their eyes met. If only she could accept, as he did, that sex was the only thing between them, the only thing that would ever be between them.

She remembered what he'd said the day before about her secrets. She was full of them and experience had taught her not to confide in people.

Since she'd been here, she'd had one fright on Christmas Eve with Vincent, and now faced the prospect of Adam hearing about her past tonight at the party. She didn't think for a moment he would be unsympathetic about the rest of it, but the killer would be her non-contact with her uncle.

Jasmine decided he should know the details— with the exception of the insurmountable rift between her father and uncle. She crossed her fingers and hoped he'd feel so sorry for "poor little Jane Cooper" that he'd forget about Stewart Cooper.

Adam waved his hand in front of her face. "Are you still with me?" That wicked, expressive mouth curved. She warmed to the crinkles in the corners of his eyes.

It would be a relief to share, after so many years hiding it away as if it never happened. Even as her fingers tapped the side of her pint glass, as she inhaled in preparation of laying her life bare to a virtual stranger, she wondered, why take the risk when there was no future for them? What if he misused the information?

What if he didn't and it brought them closer?

Jasmine swallowed and looked at him steadily. "My mother died when I was fourteen, after spending ten years in a psychiatric institution. She—she never got over the fact that she was driving when my brother was killed in a car accident, not long after I was born."

Adam had been holding his pint to his mouth. Now he set it down slowly, his eyes focusing intently on her face, and put his elbows on the table. She imagined this was what he looked like when chasing a financial deal.

Or a woman… She looked away.

"They said she was suffering from post-natal depression after having me." Jasmine shrugged, her eyes flitting in an ordered way to each object on the wall behind his head, from the stag's head to the rusty old scythe to an ancient photo of Pembleton, which she must remember to have a closer look at. "Anyway, she bore it for a few years but when I was three years old, while my father was away on business, she took me on the ferry to Paris and left me there."

Adam exhaled carefully. "Left you where, exactly?"

"On the Montmartre carousel, actually." Jasmine smiled ruefully. "Going around in circles."

Thankfully, she'd been too young to remember. It hadn't dimmed her love of the horses on the estate, and she had only nice thoughts of France the couple of times she'd visited. "She came home without me. Father came back to Britain two days later and saw the news, saw me—" she cleared her throat "—on the news, and called the police."

Being only three, the media frenzy had gone over her head, but it must have been terrible for her parents. Every European country published pictures of the "poor abandoned soul" and in Britain, her parents—especially her mother—were vilified as monsters. Her father kept the details from her over the years but Jasmine picked up a fair amount from the playground at school. Her mother struggled on for another year after "the incident," heavily medicated and supervised, but continued to deteriorate. Another furor in the papers erupted when she was finally committed to the psychiatric facility, and again when she died and Sir Nigel married Gill a few years later. Every time the Cooper family name came up, the whole sad story was rehashed, most spectacularly of all when her engagement to Vincent failed. "That was when I realized that I couldn't escape my past and moved to New Zealand," she finished matter-of-factly.

Adam eyes were warm, soothing, full of compassion, but all he said was, "Wow."

"I didn't tell you this to get sympathy but you're probably going to hear bits and pieces tonight."

"Did you see your mother after that?" Adam asked.

Jasmine shook her head. "After an argument with Gill one day when I was about thirteen, I told her I wanted to see my real mother. Later, when I'd calmed down, she said I could if I wanted to and she would take me. But somehow, we never did."

Her father hadn't been so forbearing. He refused to allow her mother's name to be mentioned. It was Gill who told her that her mother was so ill and so heavily medicated, she wouldn't know her.

"Why New Zealand?" Adam asked.

Her shoulders rose. "Fresh start and about as far away as I could get."

"Does Nick know any of this?"

"No." It was as flat and final as she could make it.

He reached over the table and squeezed her shoulder briefly. "Thanks for telling me. Your secret is safe with me."

Jasmine believed him. Then again, what choice did she have? She picked up her half-full glass and took a mouthful, then pushed it to the center of the table. "Drink up. We'll be late for the meet and greet."

After the locals left the estate, full of ale, cider and the cook's excellent afternoon tea, Adam dressed for the dinner party, wandering around Jasmine's room as he did. Although it was furnished fit for a princess, and obviously hadn't been used as a regular bedroom for years, it retained some little touches of her. A stuffed toy or two, a collection of boy band CDs, a cluster of framed photos that had pride of place on an armoire that belonged in a museum, like nearly everything in this house.

One photo showed her in front of a huge Christmas tree in Trafalgar Square, if he wasn't mistaken, dated 1994; she must have been about eleven years old. Another in a silver ball gown that still hung in her closet. He knew she was a member of one of his mother's dancing clubs for a number of years.

Adam understood better now her fiercely guarded personality. She didn't let people close because those close to her had let her down, abandoned her. Those she should have been able to trust—her mother, her lover—had, for whatever reason, turned their backs on her.

There was another photo of her with a handsome, thick-set young man in muddy boots and oilskins, leaning on a rifle. Jasmine looked about eighteen and wore a smile as fresh and open as a child's. He wondered if that was the neighbor or a young Vincent de Burgh, the louse who had broken her heart.

He checked his watch and straightened his jacket, thinking at least he'd brightened up her sad eyes a bit last month. They'd gone clubbing, sailing and once for a wild motorcycle ride around the bays of Wellington.

She'd lost her breath and laughed, saying she'd never done anything like that before. She took him to the ballet and cooked for him one night at her home. And the last night, when he'd finally got her into bed, there was no sadness or tight control, only passion.

And that, he supposed, opening the door and stepping out into the hallway, was why she had chosen him for this well-intentioned scheme to convince her father they were engaged. She didn't know many people because she liked to keep to herself and with her backstory, who could blame her? Adam had made an effort, which was nothing unusual for him, but he suspected not many people in her life did that for her. Certainly not her father....

He would keep her secrets and keep her old man sweet for tonight but he wanted something, too, and he wasn't her savior. Once she had helped to bring her uncle to the negotiating table, they would go their separate ways, hopefully after a last sensational night together. After what she'd been through, he doubted she had any illusions left about love and forever, and Adam had no time in the foreseeable future to take a woman seriously.

Jasmine came out of the room down the hall and waited when she saw him. She inspected him as he approached and nodded approvingly. He hadn't expected to be hobnobbing with the gentry and had only brought a leather jacket, but Gill had come up with a smart sports jacket that fit perfectly.

"You look nice," she said, and tucked her arm through his.

"And you are ravishing, as always," he said. She wore her rich dark hair swept back in a loose French twist, long wisps trailing her shoulders. He liked the softer, less restrained look. Her trouser suit was platinum-gray, with a lacy cami underneath the open jacket and a dark green chiffon scarf looped simply around her neck and hanging down to her waist. Emerald and diamond studs glinted at her ears, her only jewelry. Simple, elegant, classy. "Very country," he murmured as he escorted her proudly into the formal dining room. And from nowhere came the fleeting thought that if he ever was to take a woman seriously, it would be this woman….

The English gentry knew how to eat. It seemed compulsory to showcase every meat known to mankind on the same groaning table. The old historical dramas that showed Vikings and warriors at table, gnawing on a massive hock, were not so far removed from today, cutlery and table manners notwithstanding.

Jasmine's father sat at the head of the long table of thirty guests. Most were older, all of them local, but there were a couple of people around Jasmine's age that he learned had attended the same schools. She stayed close to him during the dinner and they were both relieved that her father did not mention the engagement. Adam was introduced as "Jane's friend."

As dinner was cleared away by the attentive staff,

everyone adjourned to the large room called the orangery, a kind of insulated and robust conservatory, with underfloor heating, impressive sculptures, exotic plants and lots of glass. In the less formal situation, Jasmine's attention was avidly sought. Everyone wanted to know how she liked New Zealand and when she was coming home. Left to his own devices for the first time, Adam engaged in conversation with a blustery gentleman whose brick-colored complexion increased alarmingly with every glass of port he was able to snag from the circling waiters.

"Oh, yes, I've known the family all my life," the man said, his eagle eyes already scoping the progress of the next waiter. "Tragic story, Sir Nigel's wife and all."

Adam nodded absently, his eyes searching for Jasmine, bored by the man's inebriated waffle. He prepared to make his excuses when he suddenly heard the name Stewart Cooper. He raised one eyebrow, signaling his interest.

"Both brothers loved the same woman, you know," the man confided while Adam braced himself against the alcoholic fumes wafting from his companion's mouth. He waved a meaty hand in Jasmine's general direction. "Her daughter takes after her in looks. One only hopes not in morals or mental health."

Adam turned to face the man and stepped forward, backing him up against the wall a little. He wanted to hear more but didn't necessarily want the rest of the room to hear. "Really?"

The man needed no more encouragement. By the time he was finished, Adam knew every detail of the troubled marriage of his pretend fiancée's parents. Every twisted betrayal and tragedy, and the aftermath of bitterness that lived on today.

She'd duped him. He set his glass on a passing waiter's tray and went looking for her, his mood black. He'd been set up. Jasmine—or Jane—had no intention of helping him with his goal. How could she, when there was such a bitter rift between her family and her uncle that he would probably rather do business with a badger than any friend of hers?

The English rose had some major explaining to do. He found her coming back to the orangery, having just said good-night to her father. He waited until Gill led the frail man away, then turned on Jasmine, his anger close to the surface.

"What is it?" she asked, her brows knitting together.

Adam grasped her arm firmly. "I need to talk to you, *darling*," he gritted, walking her away from the party. "Somewhere private, I think."

She led him into a nearby room that must have been an office or library, as there were wall-to-wall books. The drapes were open and the bright lights of the party across the courtyard lit up the falling snow in friendly sparkles.

Adam didn't feel friendly at all. "How long did you think you could go on playing me for a fool?"

Jasmine drew the drapes and switched one small

lamp on by the desk, but the cavernous room was still dim. She turned to face him, a resigned look in her face. "What did you hear?"

She wasn't surprised, probably why she'd clamped herself to his side all night, he thought angrily. "That your mother was sleeping with both brothers, but when she got pregnant, she chose your father because he inherited the estate and Stewart got nothing. That the baby—your brother—was your uncle's child, not your father's. That she was so unhappy with your father, she was running away to Stewart on the night of the accident that killed his son."

Jasmine held his gaze for a long moment, then swallowed and looked away. "I don't know for sure that any of that is true," she said quietly.

"You've never met him, have you?" That realization only angered him more. "I bet he doesn't want anything to do with you. Why would he? Yet still, you promised me you'd set up a meeting."

"And I will try, as I promised, after Christmas."

Adam gave a derisive bark of laughter. "Don't do me any favors, sweetheart. If he knows I'm at all connected with you, he'll probably laugh me off the planet."

Jasmine brushed her hands over her face and rubbed her arms. Her face radiated guilt. "I'm sorry."

"You're sorry." He reached out and grasped both ends of the scarf she wore, watching her eyes widen.

"Not good enough, I'm afraid." He tugged on the scarf until Jasmine had no option but to take a step forward, and another.

"I'll get what I need, with or without you," he growled, referring to Stewart Cooper, "and I'll take what I want, as well."

She tottered another step forward, her mouth rounded and surprised and infinitely appealing. "What you want?" she whispered breathlessly.

Adam's anger sizzled under his skin, aggravating him to a fever pitch of desire. He tugged her relentlessly forward, his eyes lighting hungrily on the delicate line of her shoulder exposed by the scarf as he seesawed it over her skin. Her pulse pumped and jerked in the hollow of her throat, mirroring his, he'd wager. The tip of her tongue shot out quickly to moisten her lips, capturing his avid attention. He had no idea where the hell they were, but he wasn't averse to taking her right here, against the towering dusty bookcases, not twenty feet from where her peers partied on, oblivious.

"*You*, lovely Jasmine." Adam bent his head to stop an inch away from her mouth. Her eyes filled his vision, hazed over, too dark to be gray. "As soon as possible," he breathed, watching her beautiful lips part slightly. "As often as possible." He closed that last inch, his tongue flicking out to sweep her lower lip. "You owe me that, at least."

She shivered. Her front bumped up against his,

ratcheting up the tension a little. Her breath escaped in a rush and she immediately gasped in another. From past experience, he'd say Ms. Cool, Calm and Collected was about to lose it, and he remembered every thrilling erotic detail of the last time she'd lost her composure.

Nothing wrong in helping her along. Adam let go of the scarf and put one finger in the waistband of her trousers. Her front bumped him again, all knobs and bone, soft and hard, bumping together, burning for more. His other hand circled the back of her neck as he tilted her face up and finally crushed his lips down on hers.

She opened for him immediately. He pulled her hard against him, dipping into her mouth with a hunger that blasted away any finesse he might normally employ, or that she might expect. Her scent was rich in subtle passion; the warmth and smoothness of her skin incited him to go deeper, push more insistently. Adam considered himself an experienced lover who always had his partner's needs in mind, but with this woman, all bets were off. He wanted more fiercely, needed more of everything she could offer.

And he wasn't the only one. Her tongue delved in and out of his mouth, maddening him. Her hands clutched and kneaded his shirt and she strained against him, her sighs loud in the dim room. Just as hungry, just as needy as he.

He maneuvered his hand inside the camisole and

slid up toward her breasts. Jasmine's spine tensed like steel and she pushed her front out hard against him. Her head fell back, breaking the kiss, and she moaned softly as his fingers caressed the underside of her firm globe. Heaven help him, she was so sweet, tasted so sweet.

And then a harsh white light flooded the room. Her eyes snapped open and locked on his, full of alarm. Adam cursed under his breath and looked toward the door. A man he didn't recall seeing at the dinner party tonight stood there, framed in the light from the hallway.

They stared at each other, or more correctly, Adam glared at him, he stared at Jasmine and Jasmine— after a quick glance at the intruder—stared at Adam's throat, her lips moving in soundless surprise.

"Can I help you?" Adam asked, the warning in his voice implying he'd like to help him into next week through the closed windows, if necessary. He took his hand out from under Jasmine's top reluctantly, away from her glorious breasts that still rose and fell robustly.

It was an older version of the man in the photo in her room. Adam studied his pale and surprised face, impatiently waiting for his explanation. What, did he want to watch?

"I'm not sure," the man said, his voice infuriatingly vague. "I thought I'd found my fiancée but it can't be her, because you have your mouth and hands all over her."

# Five

Jasmine's eyes closed in distress. Ian! What on earth next? And why did he have to say *that,* of all things?

Her hands dropped from Adam's shirt, trembling with interrupted passion, shock and now shame. She began to straighten her clothing, not sure which of the two of them she most did not want to look at. She felt, rather than saw Adam's head slowly turning her way, and licked her chafed and sensitive lips nervously.

"What did he say?" he asked her softly.

Jasmine covered her mouth with her palm, exhaling. Excuses clamored to be let out: He didn't mean it, it's a joke, I was going to tell you... She took a step back from him, looking over at Ian, who looked as confused and embarrassed as she felt. Her heart clenched in sympathy. She walked quickly to him, put her hands on his shoulders and kissed his cheek. "Why aren't you in Switzerland?"

Ian studied her face, looking somewhat relieved. "My father called to tell me you were back. You might have warned me. It was no mean task, getting flights at this time of year."

She stepped back from him and glanced at Adam. His eyes bored into her face, one dark brow raised. He looked ready to explode.

Jasmine exhaled, agitated. She hated being agitated. "I'm not engaged," she said to the room in general, not looking at either of them.

"To me or him?"

Oh, the softness of his voice, like a velvet noose…

"Well, technically—" Ian ventured.

She shot him a venomous look, willing him to shut up, then turned back to the smoldering man a few feet away. "It's not what you think."

"Oh, you don't want to know what I think."

Scathing, angry, disgusted. Arrows of displeasure pummeled her. Coming on top of learning about her family history, this could be the last straw for them.

Jasmine couldn't bear not to see him again, not to be held or kissed by him again….

With a last hard look at her, he stepped forward. "I'll be off, since I'm surplus to requirements."

"Adam, I can explain."

"I've had enough of your explanations." He brushed past her, pausing to look into Ian's face. "You're welcome to her, mate. I've even warmed her up for you."

Shame coursed through her and she hurried after him. Ian grabbed at her arm as she passed and she spun on him. "Why did you have to say *that?*"

"We need to talk. Your father's dying. You can't keep putting it off."

Jasmine shook him off, her eyes on the tall, angry figure striding away down the hallway.

"Talk to me, Jane."

The agitation in Ian's voice stopped her at the door but she didn't turn around. "I have to go after him. Please, Ian, just wait for me here."

He let out a petulant sigh. "I've been waiting all my life. When is it going to end?"

"A few more minutes," she said with her back to him. "I promise."


She found Adam in her room, tossing clothing and toiletries into his small overnight bag. If only he'd left this morning, as she'd intended. His face was closed and angry. She could barely believe he was the same man who had kissed her so passionately just a few minutes ago, as if he'd die if he hadn't.

"Please don't go." She stood in the doorway, twisting the ends of her scarf in her hands. "It's all a mistake."

"It sure is." He took off the borrowed jacket and laid it on the bed. "Thank Gill and your father for their hospitality."

"Listen—" she said hurriedly; his bag was already packed and he'd picked up his leather jacket— "what he said…it's not really true. It was just a silly pact we made five years ago before I left to live in New Zealand."

"Jasmine—*Jane*—get this through your lovely head: I don't care. I've had enough of your silly games and your secrets and your lies. I have wasted all the time I'm going to."

"You have every right to be angry, but—" she walked to him swiftly and took his hand in hers "—please let me explain."

With his dark glower and black leather jacket, he looked dangerous, unapproachable, but she had to try. She thought too much of him to just let him walk out, maybe forever.

Besides, she had to think of her job should his displeasure get back to Nick. Suddenly Jasmine was tired, mentally. So many revelations today after years of holding it all in.

With a deep breath, she started at the beginning. "My father has always wanted Ian's family land adjoining the estate, mostly because he's worried about developers getting their hands on it. Ian is a farmer; he wants to farm the estate. Anyway, as I told you in your office, my father needs a male heir to keep the estate after he's gone."

"Or what?" Adam interrupted brusquely.

At least he wasn't leaving. "Or it passes to Stewart." There was a long silence while he digested that. This was the tricky part, because now he knew how irreconcilable the differences between the brothers were. What use would she be to him?

In front of her, Adam shifted impatiently. She'd lose him if she didn't get on with it. "When I met Vincent, my father strenuously disapproved. His connections aside, he thought he was a money-grabbing opportunist." Sage words as it turned out a short time later.

"Because of his high profile in the tabloids, I came in for a lot of interest but it wasn't until he ran off with my best friend that..." Jasmine closed her eyes to blot out the headlines. "Everything you heard tonight about Uncle Stewart and the love triangle, my mother abandoning me and going mad. Poor little Jane, everybody leaves her, they said. I was a national joke."

She gulped in air, reliving the horror of the paparazzi at the gate, being followed everywhere. "My father was beside himself with shame." It had taken her years to forgive him for his cruelty in those dark days. "He said the only thing I could do to make it better was to marry Ian. The press would lose interest and we'd all be left alone. And the estate would be safe from Stewart."

But there must have been a bit more life in her. She

couldn't bear the thought of staying and being at the mercy of the press all her life. And she couldn't bear the thought of waking next to a man she didn't love every day. Jasmine had been hurt badly by the actions of her mother and lover, but something inside her wouldn't let her give up on life and love just yet.

"I tried to love Ian, I really did, but I just couldn't make myself go through with a wedding. I had finished my degree but had plans to work in the history field or at least do some more study, but the publicity didn't let up. In the end, I took the coward's way out. I ran away."

Was she imagining it or had Adam's hand, sandwiched between hers, softened and warmed? "When I left, Ian and I made a silly promise that if neither of us was married by the time we were twenty-five, we'd marry each other." Twenty-five had seemed a lifetime away when she was twenty. Jasmine knew Ian felt more for her than she did him, but he didn't love her, either, not the way she wanted to be loved. They were friends and he wanted the estate. "I honestly thought he'd find someone else in my absence."

"But he didn't."

She looked up and saw that Adam's expression wasn't any friendlier than before.

"It was a stupid agreement, entered into at a time when I was overemotional and just wanted to be away." She squeezed his hand between hers, imploring him with her eyes to believe her.

Unmoved, Adam retrieved his hand from hers. "He seems to be taking it seriously enough."

Jasmine swallowed, feeling him cool and close up. "I'll talk to him tonight."

Adam gave her another hard look, then walked away from her toward the window. He pulled the drapery back. The snow was still falling. She clutched at the hope that he wouldn't be able to leave because of the weather.

"You're full of surprises, aren't you, *Jane?*"

"The only lie I told was assuring you I could set up a meeting with my uncle."

"Oh, but you've been very economical with the truth." He turned, his gaze dark as night. "These little games, playing hard to get a few weeks ago, making promises you have no way of keeping, telling me half truths—I didn't expect it of you."

Jasmine's heart fell. His attention, his admiration had surprised her from the first. It was a nice feeling, and it saddened her to lose it. "I've been such a disappointment to my father," she said quietly. "I wanted to please him just once before he died."

Adam shrugged and turned back to the window. "I don't particularly like the way he treats you, but the ultimate way to please him, if you want to throw your life away, is to marry Ian." He paused. She saw him tilt his head at the reflection, knew he was watching her in it.

"As you know," he continued conversationally,

"I'm not in the market for marriage. I certainly won't stop you."

She shook her head miserably. It wouldn't be fair, to herself or to Ian.

Adam's disappointment in her lanced her heart. Right from the start she'd been determined not to get involved with him. He hadn't seemed to mind her reticence; he'd just set about seducing her over a period of weeks. She loved the attention—and the company. Even while fending him off as nicely as she could, she dreamed of him, vivid, addictive dreams that left her hot, turned on and uncomfortably aware of her loneliness. The reality, when finally she couldn't bear to push him away, was so much better than her dreams.

Adam might be a career womanizer but he'd always made her feel special, as if she was worth the wait. However, she had no hold on him now; he'd sampled the goods, and because of her actions, he was disappointed in her.

The fight left her. Jasmine hung her head, the design on the carpet blurring as she studied the floor. "I'm so sorry, Adam. And grateful, for everything." Her shoulders rose and fell helplessly. "I wish I could make it up to you."

Two large black shoes appeared in front of her feet. She looked up in surprise, not hearing his approach.

His eyes were cool, his lips set in a thin line.

"Oh, you'll make it up to me, all right," Adam said

softly. "I want you, God help me." His thumb brushed the corner of her mouth and continued slowly on along her bottom lip. "Don't bother adding to your litany of lies by denying that you want me, too."

She took a deep, shuddering breath in, hoarding it. Excitement gripped her in hot, sharp claws.

"And I intend to collect," Adam continued, his finger tracing her chin, down over the edge, and kept going to the hollow in her throat.

Jasmine's head rolled back a little, all her senses focused on his stern, searing eyes, his wicked mouth and the finger burning a path down her front.

His eyes never left her face, watching her struggle to breathe, to contain the soaring desire that only he could invoke. He brought his hand back to her chin, cupping it, studying her like an exhibit. His voice became businesslike. "I'll send a car for you on Thursday, at noon. Bring your passport and pack enough for a couple of days."

She blinked, her mind a flurry of nerves, desire and confusion. Maybe a little relief that he still wanted her. "Where…?"

Adam smiled grimly. "I have no idea yet." His fingers on her chin firmed and his smile became a scowl. He bent his head so that his mouth was very close to hers. "But make no mistake, wherever it is, we will be together." His fingers gentled and then he released her. "Don't even think of letting me down."

Jasmine tried to formulate a reply but her mind

was in a spin. The most galling thing to accept was the excitement dulling her senses, thickening her tongue, sending that howl of triumph through her blood. Not indignation, defiance, or even fear. And that was not a good sign.

With one last hard look, Adam turned to go. But at the door, he swung back to her. "There is no question you have suffered in your life. No one could blame you for having abandonment issues." He paused, his eyes pitiless. "But for God's sake, if you don't intend to marry him, put that poor sap out of his misery."

# Six

Three days later, she found herself on a private executive jet, wondering what on earth she was doing. Where was Adam? The car had arrived at noon, driven her to an airstrip just outside London, and a flight attendant had bustled her up the steps and into a seat and taken her passport away for checking. Now the engines began to roar, and there was still no sign of him.

This wasn't her intention. After he'd left the party, Jasmine realized Adam was right. She'd been keeping Ian hanging, giving him hope. Afraid that she'd lose the only friend she had if she stripped him of that. After all, hadn't everyone else let her down?

Her heart-rending talk with Ian had convinced her that she was about to be humiliated again. He'd checked Adam out, said his playboy status was on a par with Vincent's. Adam himself had told her he wasn't in the market for a relationship.

Jasmine recognized the danger of losing her head and her heart to Adam Thorne. This madness must be nipped in the bud before someone—she—got really hurt. So yesterday she had taken the bull by the horns and gone to see her uncle, telling only Gill what she was up to.

The flight attendant returned with her passport and checked that her seat belt was buckled.

"Is Mr. Thorne here yet?" Jasmine asked.

The woman shook her head. "You are our only passenger today."

"But—" Jasmine's mouth fell open. "Where are we going?"

"Vienna," came the reply.

Vienna? In one second flat, she forgot her resolution and soared with excitement. She'd never visited the city before and yet felt she knew it intimately. Courtesy of her love of ballroom dancing, especially the waltz, she had dreamed for years of attending a ball in the Austrian capital. Each year, Vienna staged around three hundred balls, and tonight—New Year's Eve—was the opening ball of the season, the Kaiserball, the greatest of them all. Jasmine nearly passed out with excitement and recalled telling Adam on one of their dates that it was a lifelong ambition to attend this particular ball.

He'd remembered. Her throat closed up. Emotions she didn't want to acknowledge rose up and begged to be acknowledged.

But she'd only come to tell him about her uncle. She had fulfilled her part of the bargain and when the car had arrived at Pembleton, she'd gotten into it with no intention of going away for a dirty weekend. Determined not to be tempted, she hadn't even packed a bag. She didn't expect a fight about it. After all, it was what he'd wanted all along. She was only the consolation prize.

The reception she'd gotten from Stewart Cooper had overwhelmed her. Far from being spiteful or angry at her unannounced visit, he seemed hungry for her company. Hungry for some connection to her mother. He had never loved another soul.

Jasmine liked him. For all his money, he cut a sad and lonely figure. He told her he'd visited her mother every single week in the ten years she'd been in the psychiatric institution.

"I would sit and hold her hand," he said sadly, "looking at her face while she stared out of the window. She never looked at me and never spoke. I think she was so wracked by guilt—the car accident, abandoning you, hurting Nigel—that she couldn't bear to see me. But I couldn't bear not to see her."

Jasmine had wept, haunted by the thought of it.

She hadn't known her mother well and had good reason to despise her. But the thought of this kind, sad-eyed old gentleman holding her mother's hand, week after week, year after year, when she wouldn't look at him or speak to him…it was so terribly sad.

Her uncle hoped to see Jasmine again. He also promised to check out Adam's business. If his advisors were in favor, he would contact him directly.

Jasmine sat back in her seat as the plane took off, her mind racing with excitement and confusion. Was Adam already there? Please God it was the Kaiserball she was going to. If so, how could she resist anything he asked of her?

And what was she going to do for clothes?

*"Danke schoen."*

Adam left the boutique having purchased the gown and arranged for it to be delivered to the hotel. He checked his watch. She would be landing in an hour. He had time to shower, dress and leave her a note. And the gown.

He hadn't been able to resist. He'd intended to take her shopping since she'd have no idea of the event they were attending. Luckily he knew a savvy travel agent who'd not only managed to find tickets to the coveted event but also, through a late cancellation, to get him a suite at *the* hotel in Vienna. Considering it was New Year's Eve, the man deserved a medal.

Quite by chance, he'd seen a creation in the window of a boutique that took his breath away—at least, when he imagined Jasmine Cooper's curves poured into it. God knows she didn't deserve it, but after all, it was for his pleasure, not hers.

She'd made him crazy with all her heartbreaking secrets. Maybe—just maybe—he felt a tiny bit guilty about the sex-as-payment thing. Not too guilty, but once he started on the arrangements, the whole thing took on a mind of its own. He was setting the scene for sex, that's all, and he would give her a night to remember.

He couldn't wait to see how she looked in her finery. His step was light, his smile ready as he entered the opulent Hotel Imperial and headed for the elevators. On impulse, he doubled back and with his rudimentary German, asked the clerk to order a horse-drawn carriage for tonight. The princess was going to the ball in style.

Jasmine stood outside the fabled Hotel Imperial, her mouth hanging open. This was supposedly one of the most romantic hotels in the world. Her day just got better and better.

The flight was uneventful and speedy—or that might have been her mind racing. The only hitch came as she walked uncertainly into the airport, wondering where Adam was. Wondering if there was some cruel joke afoot.

But there was a man with a sign: *Fräulein* Cooper.

And a short drive later, here she was, so excited she could barely contain it.

She checked in, her heart soaring when told they were expecting her, and asked for a map and a directory of clothing stores. Her head told her to entertain the possibility that she wasn't going to the ball—she'd find out in a few minutes—but she needed underwear, toiletries, something to wear tomorrow.

She followed a personal butler to the suite booked in Adam's name. He opened the door with a flourish and left her alone.

Jasmine was too awestruck to wonder where Adam was. She shed her coat, handbag and shoes where she stood, walked out into the middle of a star-patterned parquet floor, and just stood for long minutes, taking it all in. It was too much! If she expired right this minute, she could not be happier.

Opulence of a degree she'd never encountered transported her back to another age. Crystal chandeliers glittered from the high ceiling. Rich silk covered the walls behind gilded frames holding precious nineteenth-century oil paintings. Antique chaise lounges, bowls of flowers and fruit—she nearly cried out when she saw the perfect Biedermeier armoire. Everywhere she looked, a new treasure delighted her.

After an age, she walked into the bedroom with some trepidation. Surely such perfection could not be improved upon. She was wrong. The huge canopied bed somehow didn't dwarf the room, perhaps because of the impressive height of the ceilings or the massive Baroque-framed mirror opposite. Elegant casement windows flooded the room with light and looked out over the Musikverein, one of the finest concert halls in the world and home to the Vienna Philharmonic.

By the time she got to the bathroom, Jasmine's senses were exhausted but it boasted every conceivable luxury, she was sure. Plus a sign that Adam had been here, a damp towel on the rail and his toiletries on the double vanity. Further checks revealed clothes in the closet, a used cup in the sink and an English newspaper open on a sofa.

She sat on a plush chaise lounge and took out her phone, assuming he would have the same number he'd used in New Zealand. But on a whim, she called Gill instead of Adam.

"You'll never guess where I am."

Gill squealed when she heard. Jasmine floated around the suite again, trying to describe it. Finally, she remembered to ask after her father.

There was an ominous pause. "He's not having a good day. He talked to Ian who painted a rather grim picture of Adam's character and also said you've given him no hope of you two marrying someday."

Jasmine sighed. She knew her father would be upset to know there was no hope of her and Ian marrying. Why couldn't he see how unreasonable it was to try to force her in this day and age?

She snorted and looked around. What day and age was she in again?

A knock at the door sounded. "Gill? I have to go. I think Adam's just arrived back." She told her stepmother she would be back in a couple of days and opened the door to find the butler holding a very large flat box.

"Fräulein Cooper?"

"*Ja?*"

She took the box and he waved away her tip. Jasmine pulled off the ribbon and tissue paper, humming with excitement. Her breath caught in her throat when she saw the color of the gown. She'd describe it as thistle, a pale purple but with a depth that surpassed lilac. It was strapless with two ruched panels in the front, so that the full overskirt raised up, revealing lilac gauze underneath. The bodice sparkled with Swarovski crystals. It was the most beautiful thing Jasmine had ever seen. She lifted it carefully, noting the handwrought hanger, and rushed to the bedroom mirror, holding it up against her.

In the image, her average gray eyes were shining and looked almost indigo. One hand held the dress against her front while she hurriedly scooped her hair up with the other. Her happiness knew no bounds. Adam had bought her a gown. What else was she to think but that Cinderella *would* go to the ball!

But where was her prince? She remembered her

phone and regretfully hung the gown in the ward-robe. She had just walked out of the bedroom when another knock sounded. The butler with another box. Jasmine just stood there, looking at him stupidly, and the poor man had to walk past her, place the box on the table and close the door behind him.

A white fur cape. Correction, faux fur. And not quite white, a smoky pale gray. The perfect accessory for the gown.

Accessories. She'd need gloves, shoes, a strapless bra. Maybe some earrings…how much time did she have? It was then that she noticed the envelope on the exceptional Baroque writing desk. Of course, he would think with her love of antiques that she would have looked there first, but the whole suite was full of such treasures. She slid a single heavy page from the envelope. Handwritten, brief:

Your carriage will be waiting downstairs at 7:00 p.m. I'll see you by the Grand Staircase. A.

Jasmine checked her watch and got moving.

A couple of hours later, she staggered into the suite, laden with bags. Shower, makeup, hair…no time for an appointment with a *ballfrisuren*, the hotel hairdresser specializing in ball hairdos.

She'd have to make do herself. Humming *Die Fledermaus*, she threw herself into her preparations.

At five minutes before seven she left the suite,

walked out of the hotel and was guided into a horse-drawn carriage. Of course…

They moved slowly down the Ringstrasse toward the Hofburg Palace. A light snow fell, and the city glittered. Everything was so perfect, Jasmine felt she might die with happiness. And the first nerves were starting to bite at the thought of seeing him again. He had been so angry with her.

She hadn't expected him to be so thoughtful. Or generous. She'd heard Adam was well off, but this excursion must have cost a small fortune. How could she ever repay him?

Unease slipped below the mantle of joy cloaking her, just for a moment. She knew exactly what he expected for payment. But surely he knew that all this trouble and expense wasn't necessary. Her acquiescence to Adam Thorne came as cheap as one touch, one look into his eyes.

Then the lights of the palace showed through the snow and her nerves evaporated. The fairy tale continued. They slowly approached the great palace, from which it seemed a thousand windows glowed. Jasmine floated toward the entrance, along with hundreds of others in their beautiful clothes, and finally she was inside.

Lord, how would she ever find him? There must have been a couple of thousand people milling around, all craning their necks, waiting with a muted air of expectancy.

She looked for the staircase and took stock. The men were all in black or white tails or dinner suits. Jasmine moved in the direction of the great marble staircase and then, wonder of wonders, there he was, head and shoulders above everyone else, even though he leaned against a wall. His dark good looks magnetized her eyes. Perfect—except there were still about a thousand bodies between them.

Luckily the Imperial Guards chose that moment to conduct their changing of the guard ceremony and the crowd mostly stilled so she was able to push her way through, looking up every so often to check on his location. Her apprehension grew as she neared. Would he like the gown on her? Was he still angry? But she couldn't believe he would go to all this trouble and expense if he did not intend her to enjoy it.

She paused about ten feet away to admire him. The elegant black dinner suit draped his tall, lean body, caressing his broad shoulders and slim hips. With his trendy haircut and trademark stubble, he hardly fit the mold of one of the imperial family, but he stood out like an emperor with his presence and vitality. A perfectly tied bow tie completed the package. She drank the sight in and tucked it away to last her the rest of her life.

As if on cue, he half turned. His head raised, as if scenting the air, and then his eyes found hers and sucked the breath from her lungs. He straightened but did not walk forward to meet her. A commanding presence in a sea of people. The crowds and the opulence, even the orchestra faded away and to Jasmine, they were the only two people here. Holding his gaze, her confidence surging, she moved toward her prince as if in a dream. They stared at each other, his stern demeanor softening into admiration. Finally Jasmine could breathe again.

She felt more beautiful than she had ever felt in her life. In that one long look, he'd given her back her pride, her self-confidence, her belief in herself as a desirable woman. All the things she'd lost years ago. He took both her gloved hands and just looked at her as if seeing her for the first time.

A fanfare rang out and there was a hush while everyone waited for the official welcome by the actors playing Emperor Franz Josef and Empress Sisi. The spell was broken. Adam inclined his head and offered her his arm. They made their way up the marble staircase to the state chambers, Jasmine's eyes devouring every detail: myriad twinkling lights, beautifully set tables, huge urns of carnations everywhere. A silk-liveried waiter showed them to their table and finally, she could sit, take off her cape and say hello to the man who had made this all possible.

He passed her a glass of champagne.

"I'm—speechless," she said, and then, because she wanted to clear the air so they could enjoy themselves, she asked if he was still angry.

He shook his head, his eyes on her face. "It's your night, for now."

The implication was clear but Jasmine didn't mind. She was too happy to mind that she was here because she owed him. "Don't worry," she smiled. "I promise not to turn into a pumpkin at the stroke of midnight."

He gazed at her, his eyes rich with approval.

"Adam, all of this—" she raised her gloved hand, indicating the sumptuous surroundings "—it's too much. This—" her hand swept down the front of her, and his eyes followed "—and the hotel. It's like a dream. I can't believe I'm here."

He turned in his seat to face her, his hands clasped in front of him. "Tonight we're going to indulge our every whim."

A bubble of desire popped in her veins. Every muscle tightened and warmed. Adam noticed, she knew, because his eyes sharpened and again roamed slowly down her body. Her arms ached to wrap around him, to feel the burn of his beard on her face, the strength of his arms around her.

"Don't think about it," he said softly. "Just enjoy."

"It's perfect, Adam." She leaned close and touched her lips to his. "Thank you."

He gave a short laugh. "You won't thank me when I step on your toes."

They served themselves from the sumptuous buffet and watched the opening polonaise where beautiful girls in white gowns and boys in tails strutted and stepped expertly in formation. "It's a sort of debutantes' dance," she explained to Adam. "I was reading about this ritual before the major balls in Vienna that turned me on to ballroom, when my friends were all into pop or sports. Now it's my only social life."

"Poor lonely little dancer." He smiled. "Perhaps you should take up surfing or watching rugby."

"Typical Kiwi bloke. I don't dance to meet men. It just gets me out of the house."

"Perhaps you haven't danced with the right men," Adam said enigmatically.

As she wondered what he meant, the dance master called out the words that everyone was waiting for— *"Alles Waltzer!"*

Adam stood and offered his hand. "Shall we?"

Jasmine's smile stretched wide. "I would be honored, sir."

In between courses, they danced to Strauss and Mozart in each of the seven ballrooms. A Viennese waltz was much faster than other waltzes, and once it was learned, every other waltz seemed pedestrian.

From the moment Adam took her into his arms, Jasmine realized that this would be a dance like no other. He wasn't quite the best dance partner she'd ever had, and anyway, the finer points of the waltz were somewhat lost in the crush of people. But dancing with him was like making love with him. He was all she could see and feel. His eyes never left her face, bathing her in such intensity that she moved on autopilot, which, thankfully, she was proficient enough to do. She forgot about her feet and concentrated on feeling the music on the inside and absorbing his presence on the outside. His hands under her palm and on the small of her back were warm and dry and as they moved together, so did his hands, causing starbursts of delicious friction on her skin that effervesced to every nerve ending.

She remembered how she felt after they'd made love for the first time. Sensitized, energized, pulsing in small bursts of sensation that she never wanted to end. She felt his breath on her face, his muscles bunched under her fingertips and the length of his legs when they brushed hers occasionally. Her body became his instrument, to lead and spin and twirl at will, an extension of his own.

Her anticipation grew as one dance flowed into another and another. Adam Thorne exuded sexuality and could turn her on even in the midst of thousands of people. And if that was his intention, he was exacting his payment early in the evening but strangely enough, it wasn't more than she wanted to give.

# Seven

Adam could not take his eyes off her. The pleasure he took from her enjoyment of the evening was unsurpassed by anything he had known, which perplexed him because of his selfish reasons for doing it. He crushed it down in case the feeling became addictive, and then where would it all end?

Her enchantment was to be expected. What was unexpected was how enthralled he was watching her eyes sparkle—no sign of sadness now—her lovely mouth curve in yet another delighted smile as each new image or dance or bar of music registered and gave her joy.

His instincts about the color and style of the gown were spot-on. Her pale skin and dark hair and brows

lent the delicate shade of fabric a richness that anyone else would have overpowered. Dusky gray eyes
and her hair pulled back in a classic, elegant chignon
completed a picture that would stay with him for a
long time.

And yet what arrogance he'd displayed to choose
her clothes. What vanity to set the scene as he had.
But what pleasure to see her happiness, especially
knowing that this woman did not usually allow herself to get carried away.

What anticipation he had of the night to come…she
looked amazing in that dress, but he wanted her out
of it more with every minute that passed. His body had
been reminding him of that all night.

Just before midnight, the orchestras faded away
to the chimes of the giant bell of St. Stephen's as
it rang the old year away. Adam stood behind her
at the stroke of twelve and as the crowd erupted
into applause, his hands dropped onto her bare
shoulders and Jasmine turned and smiled at him.
Everyone was smiling, some were kissing and hug-
ging and shaking hands, some had moved between
the tables and began to dance to the first strains of
*The Blue Danube* waltz, heralding the New Year in.

He and Jasmine stared at each other and he saw
his desire glow in her eyes, darkening them to a shade
deeper than her gown. He knew now why he'd
bought it. He stepped closer and bent his head, keeping his eyes open.

"Happy New Year, Jasmine."

She raised up to meet him, whispering something, her lips soft and fragrant and perfect. He tasted her upper lip with the tip of his tongue, tracing the outline of her mouth, and she leaned even closer, sighing, her mouth moving under his. His hand on the small of her back tightened, drawing her close, and they kissed until they were breathless.

When Adam drew back, he felt on a more even keel, even though his breath was ragged and he was as hard as rock. Normal service had been resumed. She wanted him. He wanted her. She would go where he led, just like on the dance floor.

They stayed to watch the New Year operetta and the Fledermaus Quadrille, a highlight for Jasmine. It was late and the ball would go on for hours yet, but Adam was suddenly tired of people. They left the Imperial Palace. The night was cold but clear and they decided to walk along the busy Ringstrasse back to the hotel.

Jasmine was hungry since she'd professed to be too excited to eat much of the buffet at the ball, so they stopped at a *Wurstelstand* for the Viennese equivalent of hot dogs. The streets were packed with party hounds. She almost skipped along, tipsy on champagne and excitement, humming at patchy intervals. Adam held her arm tightly, mindful of the earlier snow, the uneven paving stones and the spiky high heels she insisted on wearing.

The drinking establishments were mostly over-flowing but not far from the hotel, they were drawn by a beautiful voice. Jasmine headed down a cob-bled alleyway and they stopped by a tiny bar where inside, a black woman crooned a Tina Turner ballad very credibly.

Jasmine pulled on his arm, facing him. "Let's go in,"

"With that smudge of mustard on your mouth?" He reached his thumb out, but thinking better of it, bent his head and licked the spot with the tip of his tongue.

In the freezing chill under a rusting old street lamp, Jasmine shifted restlessly, inhaled a ragged breath, and magic of a new kind entered her face.

Adam stilled, instantly, viciously aroused by the sudden flood of awareness darkening her eyes. All his senses clamored for more and he bent his head again, caging her face with both hands, sipping now at her lips. He tasted the piquant mustard she'd eaten, garlic and spices from the sausage, a crisp fruity hit of cham-pagne. It all fed his hunger and he deepened the kiss.

Jasmine's eyes closed while her lips parted. She was still now, but he sensed her blood, her muscles, her very cells reaching for him, as palpable as if she'd raised her arms and pulled him close. He thrust his tongue into her mouth, holding her cheeks firmly, exulting at her response as the tip of her tongue played with his.

"Let's not." His eventual response to her question about going inside the club sounded hoarse and raw.

A desperate need swamped him and he couldn't wait another minute. He pressed against her, his thighs bumping hers as he turned and pushed her toward the hotel.

Another couple entered the Hotel Imperial's elevator with them and they exchanged New Year wishes. Adam's eyes bored into her as he discreetly tugged at the fingers of one of her gloves, easing it all the way off. Jasmine leaned against the wall, unable to look away and shivering with anticipation and nerves.

For a moment on the street, she'd wished they didn't have to go back to the hotel. Not because she didn't want him—she did, desperately. But that meant the fairy tale was over. They were now leading up to the real reason they were here. Payback. She had done a deal with the king of deals.

She knew she'd be compensated handsomely. She'd already enjoyed his prowess in the bedroom, her body's response to him. But for a few hours, she'd chosen to believe she was living this dream because he really felt something for her, rather than collecting on a contract she had failed to honor.

She hid a smile behind her hand when he wrapped the glove around his neck; the spoils of war. She was really in trouble here. She liked him, enjoyed him so much. The anticipation when he looked at her, held her face in his hands…payback never felt so good, even though she should be running for her life.

He opened the suite door and stood back while she entered, stiff-backed, her stomach tight with nerves. Adam cast an interested glance at the bags from her shopping expedition still strewn around. Flustered, she began scooping them up, but he caught her hand and the bags stayed where they were.

He lifted her hand by the finger of her glove and without breaking eye contact, he tugged until the silk slid smoothly down her forearm, making her tingle.

"Shall I call the butler to help you off with your gown?" he asked, his eyes glinting.

"I think we can manage." And then she smiled sweetly. "Did he help with your tie?"

Adam bared his white teeth and hooked a finger in her cape, tugging until she bumped against his front. "My lips are sealed, but I gave him a very good tip."

He cupped her face and bent his head to feather her lips with kisses, undoing the clasp of her cape as he did. He slid his hands inside the fur and skimmed up her back, stroking over her shoulder blades. Then he settled in for a deeper, soul-touching kiss she felt all the way to her toes.

Jasmine loved the way he kissed. A complex mix of tease and command. Of pleasing himself and invitation. His kiss invited her to be passive, free to enjoy and be taken. But it also incited her to hum blissfully in her throat, to allow her impatience to come to the fore, tearing off the cape and tossing it blindly at a sofa a few feet away. She would shudder about that tomorrow but right now, she just wanted one less obstruction between them.

Again he used his thighs to walk her backward toward the bedroom, still with his mouth locked on hers. His fingers ran down her bare arm and clasped hers and he danced her into the room, spinning her once, twice, three times, closer to the bed every time. The ball continued, only to a much more private composition than Herr Strauss ever devised.

When the backs of her legs bumped the edge of the bed, Adam drew back and switched one bedside lamp on. His face fell, he sighed, looking at her hair, and then he began to take down her hair, pin by pin.

A guilty laugh escaped her. "Sorry." Why hadn't she left it down? Thank heaven the dress had a zipper and not a hundred buttons!

He smiled distractedly, intent on his work. "Don't ever apologize for making an effort to please me."

Ditto, she wanted to say, but she reached for him instead, knowing she, too, had her work cut out. Black tie involved far too many clothes—and buttons. The tie was easy but there was still the waistcoat, braces and the stiff-fronted white shirt whose buttons were not cooperative with her fumbling fingers. His hands left her hair and landed on hers to assist in guiding the buttons through the damnably unyielding holes, while he somehow managed to shrug out of his jacket and take the waistcoat with it.

He finished with her hair. It spilled around his

hands and he ran his fingers through it, smoothing it down over her neck and shoulders and cleavage. Her skin burned wherever he touched. She sucked in a breath and tried to ground herself, feeling her knees dangerously close to buckling. Not only that, but her tight breasts were dangerously close to pushing out the bodice of the dress. It didn't help when he bent his head and took her mouth again in a deep, carnal kiss, igniting a storm inside. And when he moved his mouth lower, nuzzling her earlobe, down the slope of her shoulder and across the front of her cleavage, she swayed a little, almost afraid to breathe.

"Breathe," he commanded softly.

She sucked in a breath obediently and her head cleared a little.

Adam straightened, his hands on his shoulders. "I can honestly say," he murmured, sliding his hands around to her back, "I have never wanted anything as much as I want to see you out of this dress." He found the fastening on the zipper that ran the length of her back. Slowly, slowly, he pulled the fastener down, his knuckles grazing her back, his body sizzling her front. She had time again to think about touching him, in between congratulating herself for the new lingerie. Good move, she thought, her hands slipping inside his open shirt to skim across the smooth, warm skin of his chest and abdomen. She leaned forward and pressed her lips to his sternum, running her hands over long, curved pectoral muscle, using the edges of her teeth on his nipple.

The gown swished down to her feet with a pretty rustle. Jasmine stepped daintily out of it, still in her heels, and it occurred to her she should never have walked across the parquet floor in heels. She eased them off now and started to bend to pick up the dress but Adam had hold of both her hands and kept her upright. She stilled as he stepped back, his eyes sweeping her body, ablaze with stark hunger. Down over the ivory front-clasp bra, to the matching panties and the thigh-high shimmering stockings that had—as the saleslady promised—actually stayed up with their silicone grippers, even after dancing the night away.

His head moved in a half shake, his tongue swept his bottom lip and there was a crease between his eyes that looked like a frown of concentration rather than displeasure. Jasmine raised her head, about to ask what was wrong. But when he lifted his eyes to hers, she felt again as she had at the Palace. Beautiful. Desirable. His.

He shucked off his shirt and undid the fastening of his dress trousers. Without the braces to hold them up, they fell to the floor in a pile and he added to the mess by kicking off his footwear. Jasmine bit back a smile at the snug-fitting gray hipsters, all out of shape and probably stretched way past the manufacturer's most stringent seam tests. The sight distracted her so that she didn't even worry about the expensive cloth-

ing scattered drunkenly around the antique carpet.
When Adam crushed her to him, his hands molding
her body against him, she forgot everything except
the burn of his skin, his hard planes against her soft
curves and the texture of his tongue as she eagerly
drew it deep into her mouth.

His hands stroked over her, cupping the back of
her neck, spreading the pleasure down the middle of
her back, over the curve of her behind and down the
back of her thigh. She shifted restlessly, needing
more, needing everything. He raised his head, his
eyes hooded and dark, leaving her mouth wet and
feeling puffy. He cupped her breasts, weighing and
squeezing until her world shrank to focus solely on
the soft slope of her breast, the way each tiny bump
around her nipple seemed to raise and pulse, begging
for touch. Oh, sweet heaven, when his mouth finally
closed over one taut bud, when he drew her into his
mouth and sucked. The sensation was so primal, so
deeply wrenching inside, her mind screamed
"more!" It wasn't possible to be this close to release
when he hadn't touched her intimately, when he
hadn't even touched her breasts except through the
silky bra she wore.

Suddenly, he bent her over the crook of his arm
so she lay back against him, her legs stretched out,
the backs of her heels on the floor. One arm was
trapped by his side, the other clutched ineffectu-
ally at the muscles of his upper arm. But he held

her so easily and his dark smile was all reassurance. "Relax," he ordered in response to her sharp intake of breath.

He pinged the front-clasp bra with one touch and it slid apart. *Now,* she thought, *please now, touch me…* His hand swept down her body in one stroke, taking her panties on the downward sweep, leaving her naked except for the stockings. Stroking unhurriedly, he kissed her mouth and throat, turning his head often to look down her body, laid out before him, trembling for him. Her breathing came in gasps. He held her helpless in one arm like the dip of a tango. She ordered her limbs to relax but her whole insides clenched like a vise, even more so when he began to lavish his mouth on her breasts. And all the while, his hands worked magic from her knees up to her inside upper thighs, firm, sweat-inducing strokes that reminded her he knew exactly how to play a woman.

Her eyes were open, staring at the impressive arched ceiling, wondering if this was the famous former chapel. A smile surprised her; the imperial family that may have worshipped here would not be amused at the way Adam was worshipping her. Perhaps they'd answer her prayer for release, for his touch *there* where she needed it as he circled and stroked and drove her mad. Helpless to touch him back, her head lolled over his arm, his bunched muscles her pillow. Helpless to do anything but try to absorb the millions of sensations he evoked.

A strangled pant erupted from her throat when finally he cupped her, his palm pressing firmly on her pubic bone, his fingertips teasing. The more he pressed down, the more tension built inside. She squirmed uneasily, almost afraid of the storm of sensation, the lurking torment that awaited her. Scrabbling back the fragments of her mind, she remembered her precarious position, her heels having little purchase on the floor and her mind in splinters on the ceiling. His fingers glided over her most intimate flesh, unerring, unhurried, firm yet tender, expertly applying pressure where she needed it most. And someone heard her prayer.

Her legs clenched, her throat constricted. Her breath stopped altogether. As she hovered at the edge of release, his clever fingers and his clever mouth intensified and tipped her over. The climax crashed into her, squeezing her eyes shut, emblazoning every cell in her body with streaks of ecstasy, holding her taut and shaking for brilliant eternity.

He continued to ply her with such exquisite touch until the blood cleared from her brain and she gradually became conscious of the coolness of her wet nipples, the aftershocks still rippling through her and her deadweight on his arm.

She opened her eyes and Adam was watching her, his eyes filled with dark purpose. He lifted her, his arm tensing so that her grasping hand nearly slid off. He straightened, bringing her upright. Boneless, liquid, she could only hope her legs would hold her up.

* * *

That her legs held her up surprised him. Then again, she had seriously beautiful legs, long, strongly muscled, smooth as satin. And those stockings were the sexiest thing he'd seen. Her sigh resonated with satisfaction and he couldn't help but mentally beat his chest with pride. He'd done that, put that smile there, stolen her breath and her mind for moments that stretched into the stratosphere.

He wanted more of her satisfaction, he wanted those legs around him. He needed to be inside her, all over her, to see and feel her response again and again. Her dancer stamina would be put to good use tonight.

He hurriedly shucked off his underwear and reached down to grab a fistful of condoms where he'd stashed them earlier in the bedside table. Her eyes lit up when he tossed them on the bed. She reached up and looped her arms around his neck, pressing her body along the whole length of his. She smelled amazing, her elegant but subtle fragrance mingled with sex, the sharp drugging scent of her own climax on his fingers.

Without preamble he tipped her onto the bed and rolled to his side next to her. He raised up on an elbow and fed his eyes, his senses with her. She was sensational, a vision of pale marbled skin, well-proportioned, glorious breasts, her tiny waist and flared hips giving her a feminine delicacy for all that strength. Her flawless skin glowed and was so smooth, he couldn't keep his eyes, hands, lips off her. How his blockhead brother failed to properly appreciate the sexy beauty right outside his office for five years was beyond Adam. He'd known from the moment he saw her that under the crisp business suits and severely tied-back hair, there was great beauty, a lush-for-loving body, and a response to him that drove him wild.

She smiled, a slow curve of her lips, her eyes bright with anticipation and a playfulness he hadn't associated with her before. She'd told him he was only her third lover and he'd believed it because she'd been shy and unsure, unused to showing her body or touching a man.

While he was still thinking about that, he suddenly found himself flat on his back. She rose up, a sexy phoenix, her long dark hair falling over her shoulders, her perfect breasts jutting out above him, begging for his touch, and those damn naughty stockings with their thick band of lace at the top now straddling his waist.

"You want to play, beautiful?" he murmured, sliding his hands up over her hips and settling on her waist.

"A little." She took his hands off her and arranged them by his sides.

Whatever the lady wants, he thought, narrowing his eyes. She began to run her efficient, questing hands over him and within an embarrassingly short time, he was squirming impatiently, feeling his excitement build fast, too fast. He began to count as a distraction. One elegant fingertip circling his nipples, ten nails scraping over his stomach. One lush pair of lips sipping at his mouth, the tip of her tongue delving and teasing, while he shifted, bringing his straining erection into contact with her shapely backside. He put his hands on her hips, pressing her back.

Her mouth moved all over his body, starting fires everywhere. He let his head loll back, not too far. He was enjoying the show too much not to watch, but the strain of holding back was immense. Her hair tickled his chest as she dragged her head down, bending from the waist, going lower while he went higher. His hand scrabbled around on the bed for a condom, finding one and tearing it open with his teeth.

Jasmine raised her head, distracted by the noise.

"Put it on," he said hoarsely, holding it out to her. He couldn't wait a moment more. They could take it slow next time….

She straightened and took the pack from him, slowly extracted the contents and held it up daintily between index finger and thumb. Adam closed his eyes. She was killing him in tiny, torturous increments.

She rose up on her knees and wriggled down a little so his jutting erection was between them, then tossing the condom onto his stomach, she began to fondle, light, teasing caresses interspersed with slow, firm, two-handed strokes. His mind blanked. The air punched out from his lungs and he began to sweat.

Sweet torture, he couldn't take much more, but on she went until he thought he'd explode in her hands.

He grabbed the condom and held it up to her. "Put it on," he growled. Then he grasped her thighs, prising them apart, and exacted his own punishment, dipping his fingers inside her heat, feeling her clench around him, her thigh muscles tight and hard. Good. That got her attention. Adam liked to play as much as anyone but he was wound too tight, had wanted her for so long. They had all night to indulge her playful side.

He ground his teeth as she smoothed the condom over his flesh with such painstaking care. Finally she scooted forward and raised up over him. He thought he'd expire as she eased him into her hot body to the hilt. She stilled, settled, stretched while he filled his hands with her breasts. There was something just so damn right about this, the way she looked, felt, responded to him.

She began to move her lower body in a torturously slow circular motion, her waist twisting, her breasts firm, her body gloving him tightly.

It was bliss but the need to thrust, to take, to plunge overwhelmed him. He reared up and flipped her onto her back, swallowing her squeak of surprise with his lips. He thrust his tongue into her mouth at the same time he thrust into her body. She arched up as he filled her, panting his name, matching him stroke for stroke, lifting those lovely legs to wrap around his waist. All playfulness melted from her eyes and they filled with a steely resolve as intense as his. Release became the only goal for both of them. He tried to hold on for a few moments more, wasn't confident as his own release clawed at him, gripped him hard.

He grabbed a nearby pillow and pulled her up, shoving it under her hips. The different angle was electric, deep, amazing. Her eyes shot open; she gasped and tightened her legs around him. He thrust again, taking them to another level, higher and hotter and more consuming than anything he'd ever experienced. He felt her walls, gloving him so snugly, begin to ripple. He tore his mouth from hers and watched her shatter, sob her pleasure and relief, and followed her into endless pleasure.

# Eight

Adam sat on a chair a few feet away from the bed, watching Jasmine sleep. It was after ten. He'd pulled the drapes to find the quiet streets looked clean with crusted snow at the edges, and sun shone down from a blue sky.

He'd been woken by a text from John, his friend and business partner in London. There had been a phone call for Adam from a man claiming to be an advisor of Stewart Cooper's. When told Adam was away for a couple of days, the man said he'd call back.

Adam looked over at Jasmine's sleeping face. Over the past couple of months, he'd left several messages and e-mails, but hadn't been able to breach the eccentric recluse's inner circle. He didn't want to wake her; they hadn't gotten to sleep until well after four. But it was driving him crazy, wondering if she had anything to do with the billionaire's sudden change of heart.

Not that he could tire of looking at that face. Adam doubted he'd ever forget the way she looked last night in the lovely gown, or out of it, for that matter. Now her warm, walnut-colored hair spilled over her face and the pillow, the ends twirling like gift-wrap ribbon.

He tilted his head, listing the many faces of Jasmine Cooper. So far in their brief acquaintance, he'd seen her mussed from a motorcycle ride, all conservative glamour for the ballet, crisp and tailored at work, elegant and regal last night, and hot, naked and very discomposed a few hours ago.

Jasmine Cooper with her different faces, her secrets and her very sexy body, was one interesting lady. Who would have thought that Nick's bookish personal assistant would burrow her way under his skin so completely? Too completely, perhaps. Adam could not afford the distraction of secrets, different faces and sexy bodies right now, sexy bodies excepted. For the next few months, it was nose to the grindstone all the way.

Thankfully she'd be returning to New Zealand soon. What with the fake engagement, her uncle and her working for Nick, it seemed he was becoming inextricably entwined in her life.

Which should worry him more than it did....

His cell phone beeped and he swore softly and flipped it open. It was John wanting an ETA tomorrow.

"Business on New Year's Day?" Jasmine asked sleepily.

Adam's head snapped up. She'd lifted her head up off the pillow and looked fresh and pink-cheeked. He finished his text and closed the phone. Picking up the cooling cup of coffee he'd poured from the breakfast tray the butler had delivered, he walked over to the bed and offered her the cup. "Did you contact your uncle about me?" He sat on the edge of the bed and restrained himself from brushing a wisp of hair from her face.

Jasmine blinked rapidly. "Umm." She slurped at the coffee, made a face and handed it back, then struggled into a sitting position, dragging the sheet up over her. "Why?"

Adam watched her, amused at the secretive face she wore. "Apparently he phoned, wanting to talk to me."

She nodded, her eyes wary. "That's good, isn't it?"

"That's very good." He caught her chin in his fingers. "You did that for me?"

She nodded and looked away. "I owed you."

He stilled, hearing his words, his demand on her lips, devaluing the night they'd just shared. "And yet you still came."

The tip of her tongue appeared and she moistened her lips. "I—didn't intend to. I didn't bring anything except what I was wearing and a handbag."

Hence the shopping spree, the bags he'd noticed spread all over the suite.

"You were going to stand me up?" His brows lifted. "Mind telling me why?"

She raised her eyes to his for a long moment and then shook her head.

Adam breathed out, strangely relieved. Something in her troubled eyes told him he didn't want to know why. Not now, when he had to keep this casual. "What changed your mind?"

She looked down at her hands, breathing out carefully. "I asked the flight attendant where we were going." The milk-and-roses complexion leaned heavily in favor of the roses. "It was New Year's Eve…"

Adam nearly smiled. "So you arrived at the airstrip—"

"I expected you to be there," she interjected.

"—at the airstrip," he continued, "intending to tell me where I could stick my weekend away because you'd done what I asked."

Her pink and guilty countenance confirmed it.

"But when you discovered it was Vienna…"

She gazed around at the opulent suite, chewing on her bottom lip. "I hoped…I remembered telling you in New Zealand that I'd always wanted to go to the Kaiserball."

"And you couldn't resist?"

She shook her head.

Adam stared at her, unsmiling, for a few moments longer, enjoying her guilty discomfort. Then he began to chuckle. "And here was me thinking it was my irresistible sex appeal and scintillating charm."

Jasmine's shoulders dropped, her eyes meeting his at last. Her lips twitched. "I'm not sure about the charm, but maybe the sex appeal...."

They smiled at each other. Then he reached out and caught her chin again. "Thank you." He knew how worried she was about her father's declining health. Risking his displeasure wasn't something someone like Jasmine would take lightly. "Going to see your uncle can't have been easy."

Her smile faded a little. "It wasn't so bad. I liked him."

"I appreciate it." He brushed her mouth with his. "Get dressed. It's your day for sightseeing. Anything you like."

Several hours later, they left the world-famous Kunsthistoriches Museum.

"Another lifelong ambition achieved." Jasmine sighed happily. "This is the best New Year ever!"

She hadn't stopped prattling for hours, showing off her knowledge of Austrian Baroque art and sculptures and the many other treasures in this massive museum. Poor Adam. She gave him a sidelong glance. He would probably much prefer a bar or the

Lipizzaner horses. Or, her heart skipped a beat, being holed up at the hotel with her.

"I'm sorry if I bored you." She took her gloves from her pocket and began to put them on. "I guess museums aren't your thing."

No, from what she knew and had heard of Adam, culture, history and tradition would not be his first choice of entertainment. But he'd borne their woefully quick trip to this great museum with good humor.

"Not at all," he said loftily. "Seeing it through your eyes has been a revelation. Your knowledge amazes me."

Jasmine preened a little. She really must do something to add to her degree, a postgrad art course or something.

"Like I said over Christmas," Adam said, turning his collar up against the crisp late-afternoon air. "You have all this passion for history and yet you work for a financial company, typing letters and picking up my brother's dry cleaning."

She slipped her arm through his as they walked out onto Maria-Theresien-Platz, trying not to be miffed by his summation of her job. She did more than type letters and run errands. Nick and his father traveled a lot, there were always flights and hotels to book, conferences to register for, soirées and func-tions to organize…and she realized that it may have been challenging for the first year but she could manage all of that now standing on her head.

"I enjoy my job," she insisted. "I like being organized. Nick pays well and the staff are nice."

The staff kept to themselves and that was the most
important thing. As personal assistant to the boss, she
was treated with respect and held at arm's length and
that suited her fine. No embarrassing family secrets
slipping out over social occasions.

Adam squeezed her arm. "I'm not knocking the
job, I'm just interested in your reasons."

Her reasons were completely justifiable and she
didn't feel the need to explain. She'd endured scandal
and pity and finger-pointing all her life. She wanted
privacy. It wasn't hard to understand.

"I think maybe you're running away," he continued after giving her plenty of time to answer him.
"Burying yourself in an unsatisfactory career to escape a bit of bad publicity."

"What's the alternative?" she demanded, trying
not to sound testy. "Stay in England and be subjected
to a media frenzy every time I step outdoors?"

He squeezed her arm. "You're exaggerating."

She booted at the snow crunching underfoot. Then
she sighed noisily. "You're right, of course."

What happened last time seemed a million miles
away, and it was stupid to let the past intrude on their
winter wonderland now. Jasmine put it out of her
mind. She pulled him over to admire the statue of
Maria Theresa, the Holy Roman Empress of the
Habsburg dynasty, and mother of Marie Antoinette.

"Did you know," Jasmine said, her enthusiasm for history drowning out any residual pique, "she had sixteen children?"

Adam grunted, craning his neck to look up the tall edifice.

"Rumor has it," she lowered her voice conspiratorially, "she asked her physician to stop her falling pregnant and he told her to take an apple. 'Before or after?' she asked, and he said, 'instead of.'"

Adam chuckled and patted the stone pillars that surrounded the statue. "*She's* not running away from a bit of gossip, is she?"

Jasmine laughed. Their eyes met, held and heated while insane thoughts of reproduction and birth control and Adam, naked and holding an apple, careened through her mind. Freud would have approved of the analogy: Adam, apple, sin…

Something in her face must have offered an inkling of her thoughts because his eyes darkened to a luscious molten caramel and filled with awareness. Her smile faded as an all-consuming deluge of desire buffeted her, turning her bones to water. They stood in the middle of the plaza, staring at each other as people walked around them, uncomprehending of the desire that pulsed between them.

She turned her head, looking in the direction of the hotel. They were only three or four blocks away. The back of her neck dampened with the need to get her hands on him.

Adam tightened his grip on her arm. "Hotel," he muttered. "Now."

They ran the relatively short journey without another word. The moment the elevator doors closed, Adam pulled her into his arms and kissed her hungrily. Even last night, she'd never known such burning need.

"Hurry, hurry," she whispered against his mouth as they watched the floors slowly pass. Finally they spilled out into the passageway and rushed to their room, only to find their way blocked by the service trolley. They hadn't left the suite until after midday, so the housemaid was still in attendance.

They looked at each other, panting as if they'd just run a marathon, while the woman, wide-eyed, waited for instruction. The polite thing to do would be to go downstairs, have a drink on the turn-of-the-century sofas in the secluded bar and let the woman finish her task. Jasmine couldn't wait and by the look of impatient anguish in Adam's eyes, neither could he. She flicked a glance through the suite to the bedroom—the bed had been made, at least.

He produced a handful of euros and thrust them into the woman's hand. She nodded and pushed her heavy trolley into the passage, turning to shove a bundle of towels into Adam's hands as he shut the door.

Alone at last, and Jasmine's mirth erupted in a snort. "Poor woman. She was speechless."

"I gave her a good tip," he muttered, backing her

against the wall, seemingly more interested in getting her out of her abundant clothes. He yanked at her scarf until it slid off and was halfway through the buttons on her overcoat by the time she stopped laughing.

They tore into each other, even while she wondered why this urgency, this overpowering need? After the hours spent making love every which way last night, her desperation now stunned her.

She shivered as he roughly stripped her of each outer garment, leaving her in panties and her ankle boots. With every success, as he threw the offending article aside, he captured her mouth in a hungry, lustful kiss that shook her to her marrow. A whirlwind of activity, he tugged at her braided hair, using both hands to free it.

"Bed," he ordered, turning her with his hands on her shoulders and propelling her ahead of him, stripping off his own coat as he went. He didn't stop when they got to the bed and tumbled her down in front of him. Jasmine scrambled onto her hands and knees and began to move up toward the head, but suddenly his fingers closed around her ankle. She twisted her head around and her heart went into overdrive when she saw the fierce need on his face, his lips parted, breathing heavily. A touch of apprehension fluttered through her. This was dark and edgy, not the polished seduction she'd come to expect. She fleetingly thought of how she must look from where he stood, her backside waving in the air, her silly ankle boots with the high heels probably in danger of ruining the antique bedspread.

Adam's fingers tightened around her ankle while with his other hand, he unzipped his trousers. And then he began to pull her slowly back toward him.

The sight of her nearly naked on her hands and knees and still in those boots nearly undid him. Her hair spilled over her shoulders in a riot of waves, kinked up by the braid she'd worn. When she twisted her head around to look at him, her eyes were huge with desire and apprehension. He sucked in air and called on all his powers of control to calm his breathing, needing to slow this down, reassure her. But dear God, he was riding a savage hunger.

Holding her gaze—and her foot—he drew his zipper down then used the same hand to extract his wallet and take out a condom. He let go of her foot for a moment to slip on protection but kept his eyes on her face. Then he pulled, dragging her inch by inch back to the edge of the bed to where he waited, still in his shirt with his trousers around his ankles.

Her back arched, her hands flat on the bed. He let go of her foot, leaned right over her back and slid his cold hands under her body. She gasped and tensed, sucking her stomach in and thrusting her breasts right into his hands.

Adam's body settled on hers, his legs taking most of his weight. Calling on all his shredded control, he buried his face in the fragrance of her hair and nuz-

zled and nipped her neck. She shuddered under him
as he caressed her, her bottom pushing up against
him, driving him to distraction. Somehow he slowed
things down to a simmer, stroking and kneading her
breasts until she was like a sea beneath him, a writh-
ing, moaning sea. He moved one hand down her
body and stroked her leg, from calf to buttock and
back, paying particular attention to the back of her
knee, an exceptionally sensitive area for her, he'd
learned last night.

She moaned his name, and his control shattered.
Nothing else mattered, his goals, his business, only
this, taking her, making her his, surrendering to
mindless passion and taking her with him. He nudged
her legs apart and stroked her intimately, swearing
when he felt her scalding heat.

She heard the muttered oath torn from his throat,
felt his fingers on her, in her, and lost it. From the
very deepest part of her, something broke, something that walled in her reason, her dignity, and she
cried out and it was guttural and hoarse and long. Her
body arched up like a bow, gripped in such an intense
rush of sensation, she couldn't contain it. Oh, and he
knew just how to prolong it, how to nurture the ecstasy, wring out every drop for what might have been
a minute or ten. When she finally floated back to
something resembling consciousness, she trembled
inside and out with sweet release.

He slid his hands up her arms and linked his fingers with hers and made love to her from behind. She purred and pressed back into him, depleted but eager to please. The slide of him in the unfamiliar angle, the thud-thud of his heart beating on her back, the speed with which her own excitement ignited again and surged to equal his all collided in an apex of wonder when he suddenly withdrew and turned her.

"I want to see," he groaned, plunging his hands into her hair, holding her face still. Jasmine welcomed him in again, looking up into his eyes, and then felt her heart stutter, slide, leave her adrift for a few seconds. Something nagged at her, something was wrong inside, and yet he felt so right. She pushed the niggling feeling away, rising to meet every thrust, feeling her climax rushing upon her, wanting it so desperately. But his eyes stared down and it seemed to her she could see too far in, see his soul or hers or both, and they were melding together, becoming one. With dizzying certainty, Jasmine knew she had fallen in love.

The jagged edges of her pre-orgasmic mind filled her with hope but also foreboding. But her body surrendered to a flood of aching pleasure, wiping her mind blissfully clear of anything else.

Above her, Adam became one large, rigid muscle, burying himself one last time with something between a howl and a bellow. He collapsed, breaking eye contact at last, and after a minute, she gingerly removed her fingernails from his bicep.

He wrapped her up and held her close and they waited for their breathing to return to normal. But try as she might, Jasmine could not stop the errant notion of love from invading her thoughts. To distract herself, she made a list: where they would go for dinner; whether they'd have time to visit the Liechtenstein Museum before the flight tomorrow…but it was no good.

What was wrong with her that she couldn't separate sex and emotion? The whole male population managed that standing on their heads. Anyway, it wasn't love. It was lust. People thought and said things of no consequences in the throes of passion.

She couldn't be falling in love with Adam Thorne. She just couldn't.

He shifted a little, turning his face toward her. She concentrated on the row of half-moons indented into the smooth flesh of his bicep and ran her fingertip over them. "Sorry," she whispered. "I scratched."

Adam grinned. "Always happy to sustain a wound in the pursuit of a good time."

She didn't smile. She was thinking how relaxed he seemed, how she liked that. How she must not go there.

Adam's finger tipped her chin up. "What's up?"

"Nothing." She pretended to concentrate on his arm, licking her fingertip and rubbing it over the tiny marks. "Everything's perfect."

He exhaled noisily, a sound of satisfaction, contentment. He began playing with her hair, twisting a long strand around his finger. She sensed he was leading up to something.

"Have you and Nick ever…?"

Her head jerked up and she stared at him in astonishment. "Why would you ask that?"

Adam kept his eyes on his fingers combing through her hair. "You have to admit, you two seem tailor-made for each other."

Jasmine's indignation spilled over. "Perhaps his fiancée would disagree."

If he noticed her cool tone, he didn't defer to it. "Jordan's sensational, but on the surface, she doesn't seem his type."

That hurt. "She's more *your* type, you mean." Which was a pretty clear indication that she, Jasmine, wasn't Adam's type. Jordan was beautiful, stylish, loved clubbing and didn't seem to mind her every move being courted by the press.

Adam's smile only made her heart sink lower. "Perhaps, if one can have a 'type.' You didn't answer my question."

Jasmine exhaled, knowing her indignation was justified, but a fragment of guilt rose to the surface. She thought hard before answering. What good would it do to tell him that indeed she had believed herself in love with Nick for about three years? She had prayed that one day, he would look up and see her as more than his personal assistant. But she'd never have acted on it unsolicited.

That state of affairs changed the second Adam Thorne walked into the offices of Thorne Financial Enterprises about two months ago. The heartbeat gone mad, sweaty palms and neck and complete incapability of stringing a sentence together, convinced her that what she'd been feeling for Nick was friendship, affection, gratitude for being a great boss. She'd only felt that way about him because he was very much her "type"—conservative, solid, a constant presence in that she saw him every day. And there was no question she was lonely. There were few people she counted as friends in Wellington and none as lovers.

No point divulging that former affection now, when he was happily engaged and she was sleeping with his brother.

"I think a lot of Nick," she said rather stiffly, "and I hope he counts me as a friend, but neither of us would take our professional relationship lightly."

"He needs his head read, having you there every day and not acting on it."

Her heart skipped a beat while she wondered if he'd seen right through her. He continued. "But I'm glad, because I wouldn't like it."

"Can't stand the comparison?" she asked a little snidely.

"Oh, I think—" his voice warmed "—I know who'd win that one." His finger unraveled the long strand of hair and then landed in the dip between her breasts. Despite the instant, piercing arousal as he ran his finger slowly down between her breasts, it rankled to be considered a pawn in the competition that was the largest component in the relationship between the two brothers. The anger was good because there was no way she could be in love with such arrogance.

"He has set the bar quite high with Jordan, hasn't he?" she asked sweetly, then immediately lost track when his fingertip circled her nipple. Her very hard nipple.

Adam licked his lips, eyeing up her breast hungrily. "I don't mind losing out to him in the marriage stakes," he murmured. "At least for the next ten years or so."

His dark head bent lower. Jasmine closed her eyes, accepting it. He'd given her no reason to expect more than a temporary fling.

His tongue swiped across one nipple and despite the leaden weight she felt on her heart, she shivered with delight.

"I'll tell you what's perfect," Adam said, matter-of-factly, cupping her breasts. "*These* are perfect. Feel free to scratch."

Later that night, Jasmine persuaded Adam to take a cab out to Grinzing, the wine suburb of Vienna. "I want to go to an *Heuriger,* a sort of wine tavern with a cellar. They sell their new harvest."

"So long as there is food."

They walked into a rustic tavern with a green branch tacked to the door, sniffing appreciatively as they entered. The room was rich with the aromas of roast pork, pasta and paprika-flavored goulashe-soup. The menu was buffet, the tables unadorned wooden benches—a far cry from the sumptuously furnished Hotel Imperial, but she liked the disparity—and an old man played *The Blue Danube* on an accordion in the darkest corner.

They ate a leisurely meal, followed by the ubiquitous *apfelstrudel.* Jasmine was determined no rogue feelings would spoil their last night together. They were still on fairy-tale time.

"The flight's at midday tomorrow. Is that all right?"

*No.* She nodded.

"I need to go in to the new office, but why don't you stay with me tomorrow night?"

Her heart leaped. Don't get excited. He just wants more of that crazy sex....

Adam had spent the afternoon teasing her. Miss Prim and Proper Cooper, kneeling on a bed that belonged in a museum, wearing nothing but high-heeled boots. He told her it was the sexiest thing he'd ever seen.

"Okay," she replied, hoping he couldn't see her blush in the dim room. "If my father is all right."

They talked of how long she was staying in England and when his next trip home might be.

"Will you come home for Nick's wedding?"

He nodded. "Of course. April, isn't it?"

He sat back in his seat, his healthy tan showcased by his open shirt collar, the sort of man who turned heads wherever he went. Jasmine felt blessed that for a couple of short days, he'd only had eyes for her. "You'll be best man, I suppose."

He grinned. "I always am."

Jasmine shook her head with a wry smile. "You're very competitive, you and Nick, aren't you?"

"Dad always set us against each other. Everything was a competition. He'd actually pay us to win—the most tries at rugby, the best grades." He grinned. "The most broken bones, girls… Not that we needed much encouragement. That's what boys do when left to their own devices."

She raised an interested brow. "Left to your own devices?"

He shrugged. "My parents were hardly ever there. We had live-in nannies or caregivers. Dad traveled a lot, setting up the bank in the major centers. Mum was doing the same, building her chain of dancing clubs. We saw nothing of them through the week and even on weekends, after rugby or whatever, we'd be dragged around their respective empires to amuse ourselves while they worked."

Jasmine had no idea his home life was like that. She knew Randall, his father, quite well and liked him, for all that he roared like a bear when anything went wrong.

Adam must have seen the concern in her face. "Don't get me wrong, we had a good life. We wanted for nothing and we pretty much knew our parents loved us. We just didn't share things as a family."

Jasmine knew all about that. Being an only child—especially a female—meant her father tended to overlook her existence, although once Gill came along, she had no complaints.

Adam looked around the tavern and pointed out two tables with children in attendance. "Parenting has changed a lot since then. I'm sure our generation—or the next—will do much better."

*And he'll probably never know,* she thought sadly, gazing at him. Not if he didn't intend on marrying for the next decade.

Adam scratched his head, looking perplexed. "I wonder if Nick decided to settle down and have a family because of the adoption thing."

It was only a month ago that Nick had discovered he had been "adopted" by his parents when they believed they could not have children of their own. Adam had later come along to disprove the diagnosis.

"Are you so against marriage you can't believe that other people actually want to do it?" Jasmine countered. "To share their lives with one special person and want to have children with that person?"

When he shot an interested, considering look at her, she really wished she hadn't started this.

"I'm not against marriage and kids at all," he said

slowly. "But I'm going to make a hell of a lot better job of it than my folks. I won't even consider it until I'm financially secure enough not to have to work all the time. *My* family will come first."

Jasmine moistened suddenly dry lips. Since this was probably the end of the line for them anyway, she may as well ask. "And ten years is the benchmark?"

"I'm going global. Even if that only means say, five more countries after England, it's still a year or two scoping each one out, setting up, tracking growth. There is no way I'd consider marriage while all that's going on."

Jasmine had her answer and told herself it was no more than she'd expected.

# Nine

Jasmine stared out at the dull shade of gray as they landed, remembering the gorgeous sunny day they had woken to in Vienna a few hours earlier. She tried to be happy, knowing this magical weekend was etched on her heart forever.

Adam had sent for a car and as the driver loaded the bags and they settled in the back, his cell phone rang. "Holiday over." He sighed. "Welcome home."

His expression lightened considerably a minute later when his business partner told him Stewart Cooper wanted to see him at his house at four o'clock.

"He wouldn't want to see you unless his advisors

had checked you out and he was interested," Jasmine enthused.

Adam leaned forward and conversed with the driver. "I'll drop you at my house." He handed her a key. "I have a good feeling about this, and I want you there to celebrate."

The car dropped her at his town house. "I'll keep my fingers firmly crossed for you," she told him as they kissed goodbye.

She let herself in and set her bag on the floor. Now she was alone, she indulged a girlish sort of high, waltzing around his lounge, reliving the wonderful memories of Vienna. The hotel. The ball. The music.

Adam.

She hoped his meeting went well and suspected he didn't need her prayers. He would succeed in his endeavors, she had no doubt. He was so determined with all his goals mapped out and she knew he would reach every single one, even if just to rub his brother's nose in it.

The music in her mind faded away and her steps slowed. He still had all his boxes to tick and no time for love. Could she handle this as a temporary relationship, feeling the way she did about him?

She wandered around the living room of his stylish three-bedroom town house in West Greenwich. She hadn't expected the city playboy to have a garden and backyard. Then again, he was a Kiwi and if he was anything like the New Zealanders she

knew, he'd have spent most of his childhood outdoors. Most Kiwi men were sports mad. Sure
enough, when she peered down the length of his
neatly cut lawn, she spied a set of cricket wickets
jammed in the ground.

A city playboy. Hadn't she been here before with
Vincent? Light years apart in character but the les-
son had been drummed into her. One woman was
not enough.

She checked out his fridge. Adam obviously wasn't
a cook; it was a desert in there, although there was an
open bottle of New Zealand chardonnay. Why not?
She found a glass and poured, her organized mind listing the pros and cons of sleeping with Adam Thorne.

Sex. Wow. Double wow.

His generosity, vis-à-vis Vienna. The fun they had,
a commodity sorely lacking in her life. He knew
pretty much all of the bad stuff now, the sticky stuff
that she never talked about to anyone. He was a great
listener. Quick to make her feel special and admired.
Pretty good dancer—and sexy with it. He would be
returning to his home country in the not too distant
future. And she liked his family.

She only had so many fingers, so turned her mind
to the cons, but was interrupted by her phone.

It was Gill and she sounded stressed. "No, no,
he's fine," she answered Jasmine's worried inquiry
after Nigel. "Well, not fine. Agitated. He wants to
speak with you."

Jasmine heaved a sigh of relief.

"I'm sorry, love, I've put my foot in it," Gill continued in a low voice.

Apparently Stewart had called the estate, looking for her. In one of those quirks of fate, because he hardly ever answered the phone, Sir Nigel had today and learned that she'd gone to see her uncle. To him, it was a betrayal. To calm him down, Gill told him the purpose of Jane's visit wasn't to reunite the family or to go behind his back. It was about Adam's business. "Now he's worried that if you marry Adam, and Stewart goes into business with him, he will somehow manipulate Adam into handing over the estate to him one day."

Jasmine pressed her fingers to her temple. Her plan to please her father before he passed away had backfired. Why had she lied? She sat down on the sofa and waited tensely for Gill to put her father on the phone.

A couple of hours later, she sat in the same chair. The house was in darkness and it was cool enough to make her shiver. She got stiffly to her feet, wrestling with remorse, longing, regrets.

"I'm dying," her father had reminded her needlessly, several times. "It won't be long now, less than a year."

That "bastard"—his brother, Stewart—had taken his wife. He'd ruined all their lives. He'd get his hands on the estate via Adam and once he did, she and Gill would be tossed out like yesterday's rubbish. "Beware his tentacles," her father warned, when

Jasmine murmured she was sure her uncle wouldn't do that. "He wraps them around lovingly then he squeezes and never lets go. Look at your mother."

Jasmine promised her father she wouldn't contact her uncle again. At least, she thought, until after he'd passed away.

He then started on Adam's womanizing ways, alluding to what he called "frequent" snippets in the papers about his conquests. He'd obviously been talking to Ian. "He'll humiliate you just like Vincent did."

Yes, she thought. He would. He was dangerous because of her escalating feelings for him. She'd already told him more about her life than she'd ever told anyone. She'd also given him more of her body than anyone else and had a feeling she was about to wrap up her heart and hand it to him in a beribboned box.

Her father had finished by declaring that cancer or not, he would burn the estate to the ground before he'd let his brother get his hands on it.

Jasmine's misery and guilt went bone-deep. She should have told her father the truth about the sham engagement. She'd so wanted him to be proud of her for once. But something stopped her, some stupid naïve little part of her held on to the hope that Adam would realize he loved her, too.

Two hours sitting in the dark, mulling it all over had clarified things. Who was she kidding? Her father was right, she would get hurt. Adam Thorne was not permanent. She wasn't the one to turn his head, make him reevaluate his life. He loved his life as it was, the challenge of business, the fun, the competition. He would smash her heart into little pieces, and after the battering it had taken in her life, she didn't think she could take any more.

Jasmine drained her glass and went to the writing desk in the corner of his living room. She switched the lamp on and found some writing paper. She would leave a note; it wasn't as if he'd care. And then she'd go home and somehow find the courage to tell her father the truth about the fake engagement.

Adam tucked the bottle and his briefcase under his arm and put his key in the lock just as the door opened from the inside. Jasmine stood on the other side, her overcoat buttoned, a mustard-colored scarf coiled around her neck, one glove on. Her eyes were wide and surprised.

"Sorry I'm late, it went on longer than I expected, but—" he raised the bottle "—I'm hoping that champagne will get me off the hook."

She lagged behind, saying nothing as he moved into the kitchen. Maybe she was just going out to get something to eat. Adam was tired but exhilarated and he couldn't think of anyone he would rather celebrate with. "It's freezing in here. Aren't you going to ask me how it went?"

"How did it go?" she asked dutifully from halfway across the room.

"It's a deal!" he declared, setting the bottle down on the bench.

Jasmine did smile, eventually, but it didn't exactly light up the sky. "He's with you then? That's wonderful, Adam."

He frowned. *"That's wonderful, Adam?"* She wasn't exactly jumping for joy. "I think we can do better than that, can't we?" he chided, taking off his coat and tossing it over a bar stool. "You were the one who set things in motion, weren't you?" Her uncle had been amiable but had gotten straight down to business and they didn't discuss Jasmine. "Champagne?"

He noticed a piece of paper folded in half lying on the bench, but was distracted by the obvious effort Jasmine was making to widen her smile.

Something was off. He frowned down at the piece of paper. "What's this?" he asked, turning to scoop two flutes from the cocktail shelf behind him. By the time he'd turned back, she'd sidled around to his side of the bench, her eyes on the paper.

Adam was closer. He set the two flutes and the bottle on top of the paper, then unhurriedly went about opening and pouring, wondering about the troubled expression on her face. He'd expected more excitement from her. Surely she knew how much having Stewart Cooper on board meant to him.

Keeping his eyes on her face, he handed her a

glass and saluted her with his. "To the launch of Thorne-Hadlow Investments in the very near future," he announced.

Jasmine raised her glass and touched it to his.

"First thing tomorrow, I'm going to start organizing the launch party. This show is on the road!"

Her eyes slid off his. Something was very definitely wrong. She hadn't removed her coat. "Where were you off to just now?"

She swallowed. "I was— I have to get home."

He thought of her father, his failing health. "Home the estate or home New Zealand?"

"Pembleton," she replied listlessly. "My father found out I went to see Stewart. He is furious with me."

Adam was instantly concerned. "I'm sorry. I'll come with you, tell him it was all my fault."

Jasmine gave a bleak smile. "He won't listen, I'm afraid. He thinks if you go into business with Stewart, he'll use you to get his hands on Pembleton after Father passes away."

Now he was confused. "How would I do that?" He was obviously missing the big picture.

She studied the bubbles in her untouched glass. "After we're married…"

Concerned, confused and now confounded. "*After* we're married…?"

She didn't seriously harbor hopes that this engagement would morph into a real one any time soon, did she? Adam thought she was fantastic. He'd enjoyed their weekend as much as she had and was already planning another, but marriage?

Her lips tightened. "That's why I'm going. I have to put his mind at rest, come clean about the engagement."

He relaxed a little. "You had me worried there for a moment." He tugged on her scarf. "You can do that tomorrow."

This was supposed to be a celebration and Adam had spent the last hour since leaving the meeting thinking of just how he wanted to celebrate. He knew one thing, he couldn't get enough of this woman. "Take off your coat," he ordered, "have some bubbles and let's celebrate." He leaned toward her and nuzzled at the side of her mouth.

Jasmine huffed out a breath and turned her head away. "No, I— Don't, Adam."

He was barely listening, intent on tasting her lips again. She smelled amazing, looked amazing. Being close to her put more bubbles in his blood than the very best French champagne. "I bet I could persuade you…"

Jasmine stepped back like a scalded cat, raising her palms at chest height between them. "No!"

The sharpness of her voice surprised both of them. Adam realized this went deeper than guilt about lying to her father.

He put his own glass down and noticed the piece of paper again, still under the bottle. "What's this?" he asked, tapping it with his index finger.

Jasmine inhaled and held out her hand. "May I have it, please?"

Holding her gaze, he lifted the bottle and picked up the single sheet of paper. "Why?"

"It doesn't matter. You're here now." She made a half-hearted grab for the paper but he moved it out of her reach.

"Let's see…what sweet nothings…?" He opened the paper, an ominous feeling darkening his mood, and cleared his throat. "'Adam,'" he read aloud, "'Thank you for spending Christmas with me and for an unforgettable weekend. I loved every moment. No doubt I will see you in New Zealand from time to time.'" He sent a scathing look to her pink face. "'*Best*, Jasmine.'"

*Best?* That was low. They'd spent the last two days being as intimate as two people could be, and he only warranted a "Best"?

She said nothing, her face a picture of guilt.

"Dumped by note," he murmured, his quiet tone belying the anger starting to sizzle in his blood. "That's classy."

The expensive wine left a vinegary aftertaste. His satisfaction in landing the biggest defining achievement of his career ebbed away.

"I'm sorry," Jasmine said quietly. "I had no idea what time you'd be back."

"So you thought you'd just sneak away like a common thief."

Being dumped was a novel experience for Adam. It stung, he decided. He didn't like it. He thought he'd done everything to ensure she had a good time and this is how she repaid him. Worse, he was being dumped on what should have been one of the most satisfying nights of his life. "You're really something, you know that?"

"You got what you wanted, didn't you?"

Adam's head went up and he glared at her. Maybe he deserved that at the start, the old "you owe me" flung back in his face. But what about Vienna? Not that he begrudged a single penny, but he'd paid handsomely for his demand. Her lack of appreciation angered him.

He inclined his head stiffly, his eyes sweeping her body. "On all fronts, yes." He'd never had better. The sex was off-the-planet sublime.

Jasmine sighed heavily. "Well, they were your words. You said you'd take what you wanted, and you did and it was—" her voice hitched and her eyes were strangely brilliant but Adam was wound too tight to care "—wonderful," she continued. "Really wonderful."

"I aim to please," he bit out while at the same time, images of how she'd looked at the ball, in the gown he'd bought her, pummeled him. Especially the laughter and excitement and magic in her eyes.

Those eyes watched him now as if waiting for something. Did she think he was going to make her feel better about giving him the heave-ho, offer some platitude or other like, *Hey, don't worry about it, it was only sex, right?*

She looked away and began to pull her gloves back on. "Adam, I hope we—you—"

"Can still be friends?" he asked with a lightness he didn't feel. He raised his glass and tossed the contents back in one. "Sure, baby."

His tone, the careless response to her question, the unintended sharp report of the base of the flute banging down on the bench between them, made her flinch. What did he care? It was a relief, really. Now that New Year was over, his focus needed to be on the business.

A good five seconds passed before she spoke again. "Please don't tell Nick—everything."

Her words slashed at his pride. So that was her primary concern, after her father. She didn't want Nick to know his chaste personal assistant had gotten down and dirty with his disreputable brother. As if he'd want Nick, of all people, to know he'd been tossed aside by her. His brother had warned him repeatedly not to mess about with her feelings.

Who cared? He was off the hook. "Consider your debt paid in full."

So much for celebrations. Adam topped his glass up as she closed the door behind her.

# Ten

Adam, his partner, John, and their new receptionist sat in his corner office on the prestigious Docklands site. They were open for business but, far from being excited, Adam stifled a yawn. He'd been working twenty-hour days to get to this point, as well as organizing the launch party next week, unpacking here at the new offices, hiring staff and fielding calls.

Lots of calls. The word had gotten out that Stewart Cooper was the principal investor in Thorne-Hadlow Investments. That started an avalanche of interest from some of the country's wealthiest business icons, clamoring to be included. The fledgling company's projected equity would far surpass their initial estimates at this rate, proving Adam's instincts about how vital Stewart's credentials would be correct.

"Promotion for the launch…" John said, rifling through his notes. "Everything is in hand, thanks to Lettie here." He indicated the bespectacled young lady beside him. "You're going down to sign the contract and pay the deposit on the venue today, aren't you?"

She nodded. "As soon as we're finished here. Have you finalized the guest list numbers?"

This would be a smallish but classy event at one of London's most prestigious clubs. Adam guessed that many of those who'd accepted personal invites to the launch were only coming in the hope of catching a glimpse of the notorious Stewart Cooper. They would be disappointed. The former pop-star manager hadn't been seen in public for a decade or more and Adam was fairly sure he wouldn't make an exception for Thorne-Hadlow.

He'd also invited Jasmine—a gesture of apology for his churlishness a week ago. Of thanks for her intervention with her uncle.

Of just plain wanting to see her face, hear her voice. Touch her, anywhere and everywhere.

"I have the reporter from the *Mail* here any minute for a bit of promo. Be prepared to have your photo taken."

Adam grimaced. "The offices are a mess." There were furniture boxes everywhere, his people sat at desks with wiring all over the place and no phones, and the entrance on the ground floor was wide-open. "Where is that security company?"

"I'll call them before I go," Lettie said, rising.

"Rome wasn't built in a day." John grinned at him. "Things will fall into place. They always do, with you on the job."

Adam grunted and watched his friend leave. It was nice to be given credit but it was primarily John's belief in Adam's ability to attract investment that had got them this far. Just a few short months ago, a lot of the big players they approached had run the other way. He owed John for keeping the faith.

He owed Jasmine, too. Without her, he doubted her uncle would have been interested. Once the launch was over and things started to settle down a little, he would give her a call. He'd hate her to return to New Zealand thinking badly of him.

He stood at his office window, looking out over the white disc of the O2 Dome in the distance, and finally allowed himself to acknowledge that he missed her. He'd lashed out because she hurt his pride and he wasn't used to that from anyone. Subsequently, he'd taken her slight far more seriously than it warranted.

A deep, booming voice broke into his thoughts, followed by John's voice, surprised and inquiring. Adam turned just as Stewart Cooper himself marched into his office with John on his heels.

The man who never left his house in the Lake

District, a virtual recluse, shunned by his family and denied his birthright, stood framed in Adam's doorway. And he did not look pleased to be here.

Adam moved to meet him but didn't smile. He was obviously in no mood for pleasantries. Adam thought again how frail Jasmine's younger, taller father looked in comparison to the physically powerful man approaching him now.

Stewart stopped at the desk, his legs braced like a fighter, and fixed Adam with a glower. "I came to tell you that if you marry my niece before her father dies, the deal is off."

Adam's vision deserted him for a second. He bit down on a howl of protest that lodged in his throat, and then unclenched his fists. Who the hell did this bloke think he was to demand whom he could or could not marry? If he thought that was the way Adam did business, he had another think coming.

Behind the big man, John's mouth dropped open. Adam ignored him, fuming inwardly. Damn, but this woman and her secrets were proving to be a monumental pain in the rear. He'd like to go just half a day without thinking about her.

"Well?"

Adam forced his mind on the facts and away from Jasmine's face. He recalled her saying her father needed a male heir to pass the estate on to. If that didn't eventuate, presumably the estate would go to Stewart, the next of kin. Bloody family feuds! His own family had just been through the wringer in New Zealand because of a stupid historical feud. Didn't people have anything better to do with their time?

Stewart Cooper and John still waited expectantly. Adam's good business sense kicked in. The word *no* was his least favorite word in the world but Stewart was a vital link to their success. Without his money, and more importantly, his involvement, Thorne-Hadlow would be just one more angel investment company. John and Adam weren't interested in small businesses; they were playing with millions of pounds to start up innovative companies that were going global. And marketing and management for global IT and technology required massive investment—and massive risk.

The big Englishman watched him through cold gray eyes that had similar color to his niece's but none of the life. "I'm waiting for an assurance from you that this engagement won't proceed."

How had he found out? Surely Jasmine had told her father by now it was all an act.

John moved into view behind the bulk of their visitor. Adam squared up to his task. If he ordered him out, he'd be wasting five years of planning and hard work, not to mention the fortune that he personally had sunk into this project. He had John to consider, one of life's good blokes with two young kids and a large mortgage. And for what? A pretend engagement that she—Jasmine—had instigated?

Besides which, hadn't she dumped him last week?

Adam cleared his throat. "The engagement is off, Stewart. I won't be marrying your niece."

Stewart's piercing eyes bored into him for a few seconds more then he snapped off a nod. "Good man. Nothing personal, you understand."

His entire demeanor changed in an instant and he became the affable man Adam had met at his home last week on his return from Vienna. "My lawyer will be in touch in the next day or so." He shook hands heartily with both of them. "Boys." And was gone, as unexpectedly as he had come.

"You were engaged?" John turned to him, looking mystified.

"Long story," Adam said, shaking his head.

He told himself he had done the only thing he could have under the circumstances, but a hollow feeling of distaste perplexed him. It was as if he'd dishonored her by going along with her uncle's preposterous demand. Which was ridiculous. Jasmine would not want his business undermined. And there was no engagement. It wasn't as if they'd announced the union anyway. Only her father and Gill knew about it, and maybe Ian. Anyway, she would have set them all right by now, and Stewart was certainly not going to open his mouth about this conversation.

Realizing he wasn't going to get an explanation from his partner, John looked at his watch, frowning. "Where's that bloody reporter?"

Left alone, Adam ordered himself to stop worrying about Jasmine and get back to trying to track down the phone people.

The phone began to ring at seven in the morning. Jasmine jerked awake as her father's booming displeasure seemed to reach every corner of the house, taking her back to the Vincent debacle before his illness. The return of his voice at top notch was not a good sign.

She hurried into the small yellow drawing room where her father spent most of his days, wrinkling her nose against the smell of sickness that was beginning to pervade the room.

Her father was agitatedly pushing newspapers all over the table when he looked up and saw her. "Here she is," he erupted. "My *infamous* daughter."

Jasmine's heart plummeted. What had she done to disappoint him now?

His anger at her for approaching his most hated enemy had abated only slightly since she'd told him the engagement between her and Adam was off. He behaved exactly as she'd expected and spent every minute lauding Ian's virtues.

Now, he tossed one of the newspapers across the table to where she stood. Jasmine looked down. "Poor Jane Dumped—Again!"

"Try another," her father said acidly, tossing more papers. "And another."

She closed her eyes briefly, her shoulders slumping. *My worst nightmare...*

Taking a shaky breath, she forced herself to open her eyes.

"The Heiress and the Playboy—History Repeats." She winced at the next one—"Poor Little Jane—Abandoned Again" while Gill shushed her father at the other end of the table.

Trembling, she sank into the nearest chair as the words on the newsprint swam in front of her eyes. Her father vigorously filled her in, saying that Adam had indeed humiliated her, humiliated all of them. Her uncle had threatened to ditch his investment if Adam didn't ditch her. And ditch her he had in double-quick time.

She barely heard her father's "I told you so"s as her mind sank into anguish and her heart with it. It was happening again. She didn't know if she could bear it. She'd angered Adam with her clumsy farewell and shouldn't have been surprised by any callous disregard for her feelings. But why choose the public arena? He must have known how scarred she was by her past, the lengths she'd gone to to get away from all this.

*I think you're running away,* he'd said in Vienna.

"When will you learn," her father lamented, "that love is for fools? Anyone with half a brain knows that."

Predictably, he started up about Ian again as she sat numb with shock. How Ian would never let her down, he would protect her from all of this. Finally, her step-mother persuaded him to subside and he left the room, muttering that Jasmine was as bad as her mother.

Gill sat down beside her and flicked her fingers over the papers. "Take this with a grain of salt, love. It states 'unnamed sources.' I bet no one even spoke to Adam, or they misheard or misunderstood and didn't bother to confirm it with him."

She nodded slowly, thinking that cautious hope was better than no hope, even if it wouldn't change the outcome. Perhaps he hadn't knowingly humiliated her. He could be hard, but cruel? She refused to believe she could have lost her heart to a cruel man.

Remember Vincent, her memory taunted her...

She leaned her head back on the chair and stared, unseeing, out the window, waiting for the pain to come and clamp her insides with rusty jaws. "I suppose you think I should marry Ian, too," she whispered.

Gill squeezed her arm, kept her hands there. "There's a lot to be said for compatibility, security."

Jasmine stared at her for seconds, finally seeing what she'd been blind to all these years. She grabbed on to it—anything to sway her mind from her own humiliation. "You don't love my father, do you?"

Sir Nigel never displayed affection, except perhaps to his horses, and she'd wondered if he was even capable of love. But she'd always assumed Gill saw something in him to admire. Surely they must share some kind of bond to stay together all these years.

Gill's eyes showed gentle understanding. "I married for love first time around. He left me. When I came here, I recognized that Nigel and I could be of use to each other. I could bring you up properly and manage some of the workload around here. In return, he would give me security, prestige, a little luxury." She smiled, and Jasmine's heart squeezed. "And I got to have you, honey, to watch you grow. That alone was worth the price of admission."

A tear rolled down Jasmine's cheek and Gill, wonderful comforting Gill, reached out and wiped it away. "He's not a bad man. He was terribly hurt by your mother and in his way, he doesn't want to see you hurt."

Too late, Jasmine thought. Still, there was no need to worry anymore. Her heart was dead to the possibility of love now.

All through that long day, unable to stop herself, she tracked the progress of the story on Internet sites and TV. On signing into her work e-mail address, she was dismayed to find the story breaking on the main New Zealand news page because of her Kiwi connection. It was the middle of the night there but she imagined her boss, her work colleagues, the one or two friends she had warmed enough toward to share a coffee with occasionally, all waking up to the news that she was not who she purported to be. The real Jane Cooper was so much more interesting than the efficient, reserved Jasmine.

It was all laid out in grotesque clarity: her mother's affair with Stewart, the questions around her dead brother's paternity, the car accident, abandonment and her later broken engagement. "Misplacing one fiancé was unlucky," one scribe gleefully proclaimed. "Losing two is careless."

Whatever Adam's part in the story, her uncle's actions had wounded her. She thought they'd connected in some way, felt he wanted to expand on that. But it appeared Stewart was just after the estate and his revenge.

Ian came around, but she did not want to see him and Gill sent him away. The phone didn't stop ringing. The story, even with no fresh legs to run with, seemed to stutter on: inane comments from anyone who might have known her at school, staff at her mother's psychiatric facility, even a couple of locals that had attended the Boxing Day party and who looked thrilled to find themselves being interviewed on television.

Jasmine knew one thing. She couldn't go back to New Zealand and face Nick and her colleagues. With a heavy heart, she composed and sent e-mails to him and to an international moving company to pack up her house.

Gill showed Adam into one of the unused rooms, where he found Jasmine unpacking some of the estate's forgotten antiques. From the look on her stepmother's face, he wasn't the most popular man in Britain at the moment. The atmosphere in the house was ghost-cold.

He found Jasmine sitting in the middle of a ring

of chests and boxes, with piles of packing foam and wood chips scattered around. She held a small, square silver object in her hands and was carefully turning it this way and that. She wore a black cowl-necked jumper over gray pants and both garments were liberally spotted with packing debris and dust.

When she heard his approach, she looked straight at him, her sharp inhalation straightening her back. Adam stood still, stunned at the pain reflected in her eyes. Hating the knowledge that he'd put it there.

She finally looked back at her prize. "Solid silver card case, Victorian, early eighteen-fifties. Made by Alfred Taylor, a silversmith of Birmingham."

She carefully put the case into an open box.

Adam stepped forward quickly. "What can I do?"

Her blink of surprise at his concern shamed him. Did she really think he was that callous?

"You shouldn't be here," she said quietly. "It will be worse if anyone sees you."

There was no censure in her voice or her eyes, but Adam needed to tell her it wasn't intentional, he hadn't seen it coming. "We had a reporter coming to the offices for some promo for the launch. I suspect he saw Stewart coming in, decided to eavesdrop, and then disappeared."

With the reception area in a state and Lettie out anyway, no one had noticed anyone lurking outside Adam's office while the conversation with Stewart took place. There were so many publications doing the rounds, they couldn't be sure of the original source. The fact that the reporter supposedly covering the launch hadn't shown for his appointment suggested he was the culprit, but there was no way the editor was admitting to anything. "I knew nothing about it until I saw it in the papers."

The guarded acceptance in her eyes made him feel worse, if that was possible. The weight of culpability with each new publication or Internet site or TV broadcast was heavy indeed. How could he have exposed her to this? He knew what it had cost her in the past. No matter how miffed he was at her dumping him, he wouldn't have wished this particular personal nightmare on her if she was his worst enemy, because he knew how far she'd run to put it behind her last time.

Jasmine picked up a lumpy object and began peeling back layers of Bubble Wrap. Adam paced, not looking at her, but so aware of every move she made, the way she bent her head to study the object—some sort of bronze cannon—her concentration so intense, he knew she wasn't seeing it at all. All her senses were on him.

Suddenly he whirled and squatted down in front of her. He rested his hands on her knees. "Marry me."

Jasmine nearly dropped the cannon. "Wh-what?"

"I can't change what's happened but I can make things better."

Her gray-blue eyes had a rosy tinge in the dimly lit room, suggesting recent tears.

"How?" she asked. "How could marrying you make it better?"

Adam sighed. Maybe it couldn't, but he felt so useless. "I wouldn't be abandoning you." He squeezed her thighs, not sure which of them he was trying to convince more.

"You've been talking to Nick." There was an accusatory tone in her voice.

Adam didn't deny it. Both his brother and father had called to castigate him as soon as the story broke over there. They'd taken turns to berate him for his lack of responsibility, his carelessness in hurting a fine woman like Jasmine. When would he learn he couldn't just continue to sail through life, letting people down, never thinking of consequences? Adam had been lucky to escape with his hearing.

They had some valid points. He should have taken more care with Jasmine's particular set of circumstances. His brother would never have gotten into this situation, but if he had, he would take full responsibility.

"We might be all right. We're friends, aren't we?"

They were. Not only that, but the sex was amazing. Many marriages survived on less.

"And when my uncle finds out you've gone back on your word? Your business?"

A muscle twitched in his cheek. That had kept him awake all night, but he'd contributed to this mess. He had to clean it up. "I don't think it will come to that, but that's my problem."

"Why, Adam?"

Her quiet question reminded him of all the things that had gone through his mind when Stewart made the demand. Watching the news break yesterday illustrated that he was no better than her mother or her ex. The publicity may not have been intentional but still, he'd hung her out to dry as nonchalantly and effortlessly as they had done before him.

"Because I hate that it's made things worse for you. I hate that I've made you sad. You've suffered enough."

Jasmine smiled. He warmed to see it. "Thank you, Adam," she said quietly. "That's very kind, but it won't be necessary."

Despite his earnest desire to help, relief washed through him—followed by a sharp jet of green suspicion. "You're not going to do anything stupid, are you? I won't let you marry Ian…"

Her nostrils flared. "That's not for you to say," she said sharply.

She had told him that after what happened last time, the pressure her father put on her to marry the neighbor drove her away. No way would Adam let that happen.

"But, no," Jasmine said in a more reasonable tone. "I'm not marrying anyone." She looked down at his hands, still on her knees. "You owe me nothing, Adam. The engagement was my misguided attempt to give my father some pleasure before he died."

Adam wondered how the old man had taken this.

As if she'd read his mind, Jasmine smiled ruefully. "And you can imagine the pleasure he is feeling today."

"I bet," he said feelingly. In his limited acquaintance with Sir Nigel, he could almost feel the wind of disapproval and censure from here.

"We're even," she continued. "I did you a favor, you did me one. It was my stupid idea that caused all this trouble. My fault, not yours. You did everything I asked of you—" she covered one of his hands with hers "—and more. You gave me Vienna."

She lifted her hand from the all too brief caress and brushed at her top. With her pale face and hair tightly tied back, the shadows under her eyes, she looked so much less, somehow, than the night of the ball. Not less beautiful, just faded and smaller than before. Adam's heart squeezed in his chest. He would make this up to her, he promised himself. Somehow…

He rose to his feet, for once in his life unsure of what to say, to do. "Nick said you'd resigned," he said to the crown of her head.

Jasmine merely nodded.

"Why, Jasmine? You love that job and you love New Zealand."

She exhaled and looked out the window. A minute ticked by before she answered. "I do. But the Jasmine over there is not the real me. She was just a front, born to hide my problems." She looked at him, her eyes clear. "I haven't got it all worked out yet, but I need to be here for my father. It would be a mistake to leave England at the moment. There are things I started here that I never got around to finishing." She paused, choosing her words carefully. "In fact, there is a lot of unfinished business in my life. I think it's time I faced up to it."

# Eleven

Adam checked his watch for the tenth time. Where were they? His most important guests had flown half-way across the world to be here tonight, and yet the party had been going for an hour and there was no sign of them. John and the events manager of the Café de Paris kept shooting him raised-brow looks, reminding him that the venue was booked for another event in an hour.

No one was more pleased than Adam when Nick said they were coming. He'd made a flip comment like he was just keeping an eye on his investment, but Adam knew his brother was behind him all the way. It hadn't been as difficult as he'd imagined, going cap in hand to Thorne Financial Enterprises and asking them to underwrite the new company's debt, should some or all of his big investors pull out.

"Why would they do that?" Nick had asked.

"Because I'm going to tell Stewart Cooper that he can stick his investment where the sun doesn't shine," Adam had replied.

After leaving Jasmine last week, he knew he'd missed a golden opportunity. He'd needed a little more time to get used to the idea that he loved her. Some last-gasp vestige of confirmed bachelorhood had its claws into him still. She'd have been nuts to accept his pathetic proposal.

"The natives are getting restless," John said at his elbow.

With a last look around, Adam followed his friend to the front of the gathering. Sure, he was disappointed Nick hadn't made it but that was nothing compared to his disappointment that Jasmine hadn't showed. Hardly surprising, given the media contingent here.

As he stepped up onto the small stage, he ran his fingers over the tiny box in his pocket. Before the night was out, he'd have a private audience with her, and the second chance he hoped her generous nature would allow him.

Someone handed him a microphone and he called for quiet.

"I'm Adam Thorne, and this—" Adam clapped a hand on his partner's shoulder "—is John Hadlow.

We are pleased to welcome you all to the international launch of Thorne-Hadlow Investments."

He looked out over the sea of heads at the business icons, friends and invited media, and launched into his well-rehearsed speech. He was midway through when he caught sight of his brother and father right at the back and breathed a sigh of relief.

"There are many people to thank. It's been a long road, but without my family's support, and that of a few select friends, we wouldn't be here today."

He finished his short speech and stepped back so John could say a few words. His former mentor, Derek Bayley of Croft, Croft and Bayley, was next and that concluded the formalities. The hundred guests continued to graze on the food and drink provided and Adam began to work his way through the crowd of well-wishers to the back of the room, simmering with impatience. He'd say a quick hello and then flag the family meal he'd arranged downstairs in favor of a couple of hours' drive and some unfinished business at Pembleton Estate. This time he would do it properly, give her reasons she could live with.

A plethora of camera flashes lit up the back of the room. Adam craned his neck and saw the tall figures of Nick and his father, head and shoulders above the throng of people. A swish of gold fabric and blond ringlets by Nick's shoulder confirmed the photographic interest. Nick's fiancée, Jordan Lake, stopped traffic wherever she went.

Adam stopped abruptly, his eyes snagged on a deep-red off-the-shoulder dress, close to his father. He stretched tall, but with half the crowd turning and moving to see what the fuss was about, he could only pick out parts—long, blood-red baubles at her ears, a flash of white teeth, glossy dark hair pulled back in a stylish twist. The cameras flashed again and Adam's heart gave him a kick.

Jasmine. A strong impulse to melt into the crowd and escape gripped him. Was he ready for this? Matrimony? Love? It went totally against his life plan, the goals he'd set, his vision of his future. All the valid reasons why not had hammered through his brain at regular intervals for days.

The crowd noise around him hushed and the people in front stepped aside, their eyes moving between him and Jasmine with fascinated expressions. Adam stood as if in the spotlight, wishing he were anywhere else in the world, until she half turned and saw him.

A small, uncertain smile played across her face. Adam's heart slowed and swelled and for the first time since the day he met her, he felt at peace.

It was hard not to make a dramatic entrance at the Café de Paris; the opulent decor, impressive staircases and air of grandeur demanded it. Jasmine forced herself to hold her head high but in reality, if she wasn't firmly supported by Randall on one side and Nick and Jordan on the other, she would have bolted at the first camera flash. As it was, she sagged at the second.

"I'm right here, girl," Randall rumbled in her ear, holding her arm firmly. On the other side, Jordan's eye-catching beauty and vivacity pulled a few of the cameras off her face, for which Jasmine was grateful.

They were late. That was her fault. She'd argued loud and long against going, but her surprise visitors to Pembleton wouldn't take no for an answer. They'd caught most of Adam's speech but she barely heard a word. The pain was too raw, her nerves stretched to breaking at the prospect of more denigrating publicity in tomorrow's press.

She had spent the last week keeping busy to take her mind off Adam and his kind-hearted marriage proposal. This afternoon, Nick had looked over the business plan she'd put together for the bank and pronounced it excellent. She'd spent hours working on her lists, talking to her father and Gill and prioritizing the multiple ways to best drag Pembleton into the twenty-first century.

As Adam stepped down from the dais and headed in their direction, she thought how ironic that he had offered the thing she wanted most—marriage to him—and she had turned him down. Accepting his proposal, born of guilt and pity, would be as bad as accepting Ian, who only wanted her for the estate. Jasmine vowed to forget about love, marriage and children and concentrate on her father in the short term and Pembleton in the long.

Suddenly the crowd parted and Adam walked toward them, tall, confident, larger than life, and his eyes on her face. She forced herself to breathe, told herself over and over that she could do this, she could be friends with him on this auspicious occasion. But oh, it would be so much easier in a less public forum, without oafish reporters loudly querying the current status of their relationship and cameras going off left, right and center.

In the interests of public relations, she offered him a smile and he smiled back and ran his hand down her arm. "I'm glad you came," he murmured in her ear, leaning close.

"Shall we go?" Adam turned to the others. "I've booked a table downstairs." He glanced at Jasmine. "It will be quieter down there."

They ate a relatively private dinner with a couple of Adam's friends and the family. Randall was, as usual, the loudest and best company. Jasmine warmed to see how he had taken to his daughter-in-law-to-be. After all the angst between Randall and Jordan's father, Syrius, she could scarcely believe how close they'd become in such a short time.

But as soon as dessert was cleared away, Nick began yawning and making jet lag excuses, belaboring the point so much that Jasmine quickly saw through his act; her boss was determined that she and Adam be left alone. Maybe he hoped Adam could talk her into coming back to work.

The Thornes and entourage left. Adam put her coat around her shoulders and suggested a walk. The night was crisp and cold, with no wind.

"Uncle Stewart didn't come?" she asked, pulling her gloves on as they began to walk slowly toward nearby Trafalgar Square.

Adam shook his head. "I didn't expect him to."

A phone call from her uncle a couple of days ago had thrown Jasmine into a quandary. She had made a promise to her father, but Stewart begged her to come. The old man felt terrible about the publicity he'd unwittingly sparked.

While speaking to him, she realized that he was lonely and wanted nothing more than to belong to a family. Now she told Adam a little of Stewart's history. "His father kicked him out of home very young because he wanted a career in the music industry, not the done thing for an English country gentleman."

Her uncle had discovered and managed what became one of the world's biggest glam rock bands in the seventies. The predecessors of punk, glam rock bands were the outcasts of the music industry with their makeup and glitter and rocky ballads, but a handful of artists had huge success. "He met my mother in the mid-seventies when he was riding high," she continued. "Naturally her parents hated her going out with someone so anti-establishment, so they had to sneak around and she pretended to be going out with my father instead. And then she got pregnant and my father married her."

"Did he know who the father was?"

"I've never had the nerve to ask him," Jasmine said quietly. Talking about personal matters was not the done thing around her father. "Stewart lost everything, his own family, the love of his life, his son. I'm not surprised he's bitter. He's so alone."

"Are you going to keep in touch?"

Jasmine nodded. "Yes, but I'll have to be discreet. I don't want to upset my father. He'll never make his peace with Stewart now."

"You don't know that. By all accounts, Dad and Syrius are making an effort for Nick and Jordan's sake. Enough, at least, to sit down together at a family engagement dinner."

Jordan had told her as much. Syrius and Randall had been close friends before the accident that had put Syrius's wife in a wheelchair and robbed him of his son.

They walked onto Trafalgar Square, her eyes automatically gravitating to where the Christmas tree had been until a few days ago. She sighed. Another year older, but wiser? She didn't think so.

She clapped her cold hands together. "I've broached the possibility of Stewart coming to live at Pembleton when Father passes away—provided Gill agrees, of course. I feel disloyal but…it was Stewart's home, too, you know? I feel he has as much right to be there as I do."

Her uncle had no intention of kicking her and Gill out after her father died, even though she had failed to marry and provide a male heir. She glanced sideways at Adam. Best not to mention the word *marriage* in present company.

Adam pursed his lips thoughtfully. "What did he say?"

Jasmine's eyes misted with emotion. Stewart had nearly wept when she'd asked him. "He would dearly love to see Pembleton again. I think he would enjoy being involved and I could certainly use the help."

She'd told Adam over dinner about the improvements she'd instigated in the redevelopment of Pembleton Estate. She had already hired the contractors to develop the golf course. The events program could wait for now while she concentrated on setting up the new Antiques Center.

"I've asked him to tell me about my mother, let me get to know her through his eyes, because I never really knew her at all."

Stewart had said he would gladly oblige in return for having the pleasure of watching Jasmine's children grow, but she decided Adam didn't need to know that.

"And is he going to tell you about your mother?" he asked.

She nodded. "Maybe it will fill a hole in both our lives."

Jasmine recognized that she'd closed herself off from the world, afraid of reaching out to people. Perhaps that stemmed from her mother's abandonment, perhaps not, but she knew she had some growing to do.

Adam stopped and leaned against one of the famous lion bronzes, flanking Nelson's Column. "I think you'll be very happy there, amongst all your old relics."

"I'm going to try," Jasmine said.

He was right about her passion for history. Pembleton could be her museum. It would take years to unpack, catalogue and restore the treasures packed away. Now that she'd resigned and made arrangements to pack up her Wellington house and put it on the market, she needed to keep busy and to heal her heart. That particular relic would be packed away safely, perhaps never to be exhibited again.

Given her love for the man watching her right now, that was a bleak prospect. Feeling the need to lighten the mood, she craned her neck and peered up the length of Nelson's Column.

"Do you know why some rum is called Nelson's Blood?"

Adam shook his head, looking interested. Jasmine admired his tolerance for her historical prattling.

"When Admiral Nelson was killed," she began, "the ship's officers preserved the body in the crew's vat of rum and halted their rations. But when they got to England, they found the body well preserved but the vat empty. Unbeknown to the officers, the crew hadn't liked giving up their daily tot and so had drilled holes in the vat to get at their rum."

Adam pulled a face. "Well, that's certainly set the scene for romance."

Jasmine tilted her head but her query died on her lips when his eyes locked onto hers and became serious.

Her heartbeat began to rattle. Oh, please, not another of those great, addictive surges of longing. She'd tried sleeping with him without losing her heart. It hadn't worked.

Adam reached out and took her hand in his. "Marry me, Jasmine," he said simply.

Jasmine closed her eyes, cherishing the words but wishing that they came from his heart and not some warped sense of responsibility.

"We've been here before." She sighed.

"No," he murmured. "We haven't."

When she opened her eyes, Adam stood in front of her, holding a tiny red box. Her mind howled foul—it was unfair of him to tempt her so much when she was at her weakest. Inhaling, she called on all of her composure to crush the surge of hope that burst within her. With more poise than she knew she possessed, Jasmine raised her eyes to his, but could do nothing about the hitch in her breathing.

"Adam, we discussed this. I won't marry for the wrong reasons. Otherwise why not just marry Ian and be done with it?"

Adam squeezed her gloved hand. "What about

the right reasons?" He paused and then inhaled deeply, working up to something. The pressure on her hand increased. "Such as love?"

Jasmine blinked and felt frozen in time. Was he saying that he loved her?

He held out the box. "Open it."

She eyed it almost fearfully, then shook her head. There was too much longing, too much dashed hope for her to take that step.

He opened it. She tried, she really did, not to look at it. Instead, she searched his face, looking in vain for sympathy, the anguish and guilt she'd seen a few days ago. There was only strain etched around his mouth and his serious, waiting eyes.

She looked down and blinked several times. The stone was huge, a perfect cushion-cut diamond surrounded by smaller round diamonds. The band was handcrafted platinum, delicately millegrained around the square shoulders. It was a true Edwardian antique or at least, manufactured to a very high standard of reproduction. Either way, it was the most beautiful ring she'd ever seen.

She ghosted a step closer, unable to take her eyes off it.

Adam cleared his throat. "Jasmine, last week I couldn't say the right words. I would never marry anyone I wasn't head over heels about. But I made a real mess of it and you were quite right to turn me down."

She looked into his eyes and saw that he was completely serious. The tension overwhelmed her; the desire to believe him was immense. After all the secrets and games between them, could it be true that Adam Thorne wanted her for no other reason than love?

Adam lowered his arm and as he did, the ring box snapped shut. Jasmine couldn't help the tiny moan of protest and longing that slipped out.

He noticed. Smiling, he lifted her hand and wrapped her fingers around the box, covering both with his hand. She looked up at him and opened her mouth to speak, but he put his index finger on her lips. "Just let me get this out."

He was nervous, she realized incredulously. She had to bite her lip not to smile, not to pat his arm and tell him he was doing fine. Amazingly, wonderfully fine.

"I wanted you at first because you were so—cool and unattainable. And because Nick said I couldn't." A quick smile flashed over his face. "I like needling Nick. But then I got to know you, all your secrets and intrigues, all the sadness and disappointments. And then, Vienna."

"Vienna." Jasmine sighed against his finger. Where she had free-fallen into orgasm and the explosive knowledge that she loved him desperately at the very same instant.

"I agreed to Stewart's demand because my pride was hurt," Adam continued, "knowing deep down that it was wrong, it wasn't what I wanted to do. But I couldn't get my head around it. I mean, what engagement? It was a sham, and anyway, you'd finished with me. There were other valid reasons but I knew—I knew I'd let you down just like your mother and just like your ex. And I knew it would come back to haunt me."

Jasmine's heart went out to him, humbled that he, too, had suffered so much.

"After the publicity hit, I felt that marriage was the right—the only—thing to offer, but still I couldn't admit to myself, let alone you, that I loved you. I'm so sorry for that."

"I so very nearly said yes." Jasmine exhaled sadly and reached up to place her hand on his cheek. The leather glove against his stubble scraped dully. "It's not like I have high expectations. But I love you so much, I couldn't stand to tie you into a marriage because you pitied me."

There was no guilt or pity in his eyes now. He turned his head and pressed his lips against her fingers. "Then say yes, because love is the right reason, the only reason."

His hand squeezed hers around the jewelry box, reminding her of its presence. Joy and hope, waiting in the wings for so long, began to fill and warm her from top to toe. Yet, caution—an innate part of her nature these last few years—still whispered questions in her mind. "And Stewart? Maybe I can talk to him?"

"I've talked to him already, told him that's not the way I do business. He's thinking about it. In the meantime, I've asked Nick to underwrite the debt if the other investors pull out. It's a risk I'm prepared—and equipped—to take."

Jasmine's mouth dropped open. "You asked Nick for help?"

"He didn't mention it?"

She shook her head, full of wonder.

"Probably still in shock," Adam said, smiling.

For Adam Thorne to ask his brother for help was unbelievable. Nick was the very last person in the world Adam would admit to that maybe, just maybe, he didn't have the deck stacked. "That must have cost you."

"You have no idea." He ran a hand along his brow.

Jasmine liked his family so much. When she'd refused point-blank to go to the launch tonight, Nick had pulled rank quite forcefully.

"You haven't worked out your notice," he'd warned. "That still makes me your boss. Now, get dressed!"

Now she smiled at his brother. "I get the impression Nick wants me back at work."

"Nick will like the idea of you as his sister-in-law better, trust me," Adam told her confidently.

Nick's sister-in-law. It sounded wonderful.

Just one more thing stopped her from giving in to the impulse to jump on him and scream her delight, and get that gorgeous ring on her finger before he changed his mind—or they were mugged. "Where would we live?"

"There is room at that dusty old manor for me, isn't there?"

"Of course." She blinked. "But you always intended on going home, setting up there."

He nodded. "There will be some teething problems, especially initially. I know I said I wanted everything perfect before I married, but we can work out these things over time." He took both her hands. "All I know is, you need to be at Pembleton for now, and I need to be with you."

"It's not like we don't have support, good support, here and in New Zealand," she agreed. Gill was very capable if given direction and when her father passed, there would be Stewart. "I think a wedding will perk Father up, give him something extra to mutter about."

Adam pulled her into his front, their hands in between them. "As soon as you like," he said solemnly. "Sooner."

Then he bent close. "I think it's customary in deals of this nature to seal the contract with a kiss."

They kissed, a long sweet kiss, full of friendship and forgiveness, hope and love. Jasmine felt the remnants of her reserve and caution melt away.

"Just one thing worries me."

He pulled back, putting on a long-suffering look.

"You like excitement. Fast cars. Clubs and fine food. Travel and stock-market drama." She cocked her head. "Isn't playing an English gentleman in the countryside going to be rather tame?"

Adam all but rolled his eyes at her. In reply, he pulled her glove off and she watched, thrilled to bits as he slid the beautiful ring onto her finger.

"Let's see," Adam murmured, holding her hand up and bending each finger closed as he ticked off his points. "Fake engagements. Royal fiancé's. A scandalous past. An eccentric billionaire." He paused, but Jasmine was too caught up in the glitter of the diamond on her hand to notice.

"The sight of you in nothing but ankle boots on an antique canopied bed…"

She glanced up at his face, his wonderful, loving smile, and matched it with one of her own.

Adam squeezed her fingers. "Jasmine Cooper, if you promise to try and make life marginally less frenetic, I promise to love, cherish and try my best to keep up with you."

\* \* \* \* \*

*Celebrate 60 years of pure reading*
*pleasure with Harlequin®!*

To commemorate the event, Silhouette Special
Edition invites you to Ashley O'Ballivan's bed-
and-breakfast in the small town of Stone Creek.
The beautiful innkeeper will have her hands
full caring for her old flame Jack McCall. He's
on the run and recovering from a mysterious
illness, but that won't stop him from trying to
win Ashley back.

*Enjoy an exclusive glimpse of Linda Lael Miller's*
*AT HOME IN STONE CREEK.*
*Available in November 2009*
*from Silhouette Special Edition®.*

The helicopter swung abruptly sideways in a dizzying arch, setting Jack McCall's fever-ravaged brain spinning.

His friend's voice sounded tinny, coming through the earphones. "You belong in a hospital," he said. "Not some backwater bed-and-breakfast."

All Jack really knew about the virus raging through his system was that it wasn't contagious, and there was no known treatment for it besides a lot of rest and quiet. "I don't like hospitals," he responded, hoping he sounded like his normal self. "They're full of sick people."

Vince Griffin chuckled but it was a dry sound,

rough at the edges. "What's in Stone Creek, Arizona?" he asked. "Besides a whole lot of nothin'?"

Ashley O'Ballivan was in Stone Creek, and she was a whole lot of somethin', but Jack had neither the strength nor the inclination to explain. After the way he'd ducked out six months before, he didn't expect a welcome, knew he didn't deserve one. But Ashley, being Ashley, would take him in whatever her misgivings.

He had to get to Ashley; he'd be all right.

He closed his eyes, letting the fever swallow him.

There was no telling how much time had passed when he became aware of the chopper blades slowing overhead. Dimly, he saw the private ambulance waiting on the airfield outside of Stone Creek; it seemed that twilight had descended.

Jack sighed with relief. His clothes felt clammy against his flesh. His teeth began to chatter as two figures unloaded a gurney from the back of the ambulance and waited for the blades to stop.

"Great," Vince remarked, unsnapping his seat belt. "Those two look like volunteers, not real EMTs."

The chopper bounced sickeningly on its runners, and Vince, with a shake of his head, pushed open his door and jumped to the ground, head down.

Jack waited, wondering if he'd be able to stand on his own. After fumbling unsuccessfully with the buckle on his seat belt, he decided not.

When it was safe the EMTs approached, following Vince, who opened Jack's door.

His old friend Tanner Quinn stepped around Vince, his grin not quite reaching his eyes.

"You look like hell warmed over," he told Jack cheerfully.

"Since when are you an EMT?" Jack retorted.

Tanner reached in, wedged a shoulder under Jack's right arm and hauled him out of the chopper. His knees immediately buckled, and Vince stepped up, supporting him on the other side.

"In a place like Stone Creek," Tanner replied, "everybody helps out."

They reached the wheeled gurney, and Jack found himself on his back.

Tanner and the second man strapped him down, a process that brought back a few bad memories.

"Is there even a hospital in this place?" Vince asked irritably from somewhere in the night.

"There's a pretty good clinic over in Indian Rock," Tanner answered easily, "and it isn't far to Flagstaff." He paused to help his buddy hoist Jack and the gurney into the back of the ambulance. "You're in good hands, Jack. My wife is the best veterinarian in the state."

Jack laughed raggedly at that.

Vince muttered a curse.

Tanner climbed into the back beside him, perched on some kind of fold-down seat. The other man shut the doors.

"You in any pain?" Tanner said as his partner climbed into the driver's seat and started the engine.

"No." Jack looked up at his oldest and closest friend and wished he'd listened to Vince. Ever since he'd come down with the virus—a week after snatching a five-year-old girl back from her noncustodial parent, a small-time Colombian drug dealer—he hadn't been able to think about anyone or anything but Ashley. When he *could* think, anyway.

Now, in one of the first clearheaded moments he'd experienced since checking himself out of Bethesda the day before, he realized he might be making a major mistake. Not by facing Ashley—he owed her that much and a lot more. No, he could be putting her in danger, putting Tanner and his daughter and his pregnant wife in danger, too.

"I shouldn't have come here," he said, keeping his voice low.

Tanner shook his head, his jaw clamped down hard as though he was irritated by Jack's statement.

"This is where you belong," Tanner insisted. "If you'd had sense enough to know that six months ago, old buddy, when you bailed on Ashley without so much as a fare-thee-well, you wouldn't be in this mess."

*Ashley.* The name had run through his mind a million times in those six months, but hearing somebody say it out loud was like having a fist close around his insides and squeeze hard.

Jack couldn't speak.

Tanner didn't press for further conversation.

The ambulance bumped over country roads, finally hitting smooth blacktop.

"Here we are," Tanner said. "Ashley's place."

\* \* \* \* \*

*Will Jack be able to patch things up with Ashley,*
*or will his past put the woman he loves in*
*harm's way?*
*Find out in*
*AT HOME IN STONE CREEK*
*by Linda Lael Miller.*
*Available November 2009*
*from Silhouette Special Edition®.*

This November,
Silhouette Special Edition®
brings you

*NEW YORK TIMES*
BESTSELLING AUTHOR

# LINDA LAEL
# MILLER

*At Home in*
## Stone Creek

*Available in November*
*wherever books are sold.*

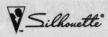
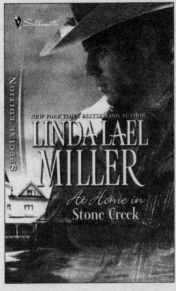

# REQUEST YOUR FREE BOOKS!

## 2 FREE NOVELS PLUS 2 FREE GIFTS!

### Passionate, Powerful, Provocative!

**YES!** Please send me 2 FREE Silhouette Desire® novels and my 2 FREE gifts (gifts are worth about $10). After receiving them, if I don't wish to receive any more books, I can return the shipping statement marked "cancel". If I don't cancel, I will receive 6 brand-new novels every month and be billed just $4.05 per book in the U.S. or $4.74 per book in Canada. That's a savings of almost 15% off the cover price! It's quite a bargain! Shipping and handling is just 50¢ per book.* I understand that accepting the 2 free books and gifts places me under no obligation to buy anything. I can always return a shipment and cancel at any time. Even if I never buy another book, the two free books and gifts are mine to keep forever.

225 SDN EYMS   326 SDN EYM4

| Name | (PLEASE PRINT) | |
|---|---|---|
| Address | | Apt. # |
| City | State/Prov. | Zip/Postal Code |

Signature (if under 18, a parent or guardian must sign)

**Mail to the Silhouette Reader Service:**
**IN U.S.A.:** P.O. Box 1867, Buffalo, NY 14240-1867
**IN CANADA:** P.O. Box 609, Fort Erie, Ontario L2A 5X3

Not valid to current subscribers of Silhouette Desire books.

**Want to try two free books from another line?**
**Call 1-800-873-8635 or visit www.morefreebooks.com.**

* Terms and prices subject to change without notice. Prices do not include applicable taxes. Sales tax applicable in N.Y. Canadian residents will be charged applicable provincial taxes and GST. Offer not valid in Quebec. This offer is limited to one order per household. All orders subject to approval. Credit or debit balances in a customer's account(s) may be offset by any other outstanding balance owed by or to the customer. Please allow 4 to 6 weeks for delivery. Offer available while quantities last.

**Your Privacy:** Silhouette Books is committed to protecting your privacy. Our Privacy Policy is available online at www.eHarlequin.com or upon request from the Reader Service. From time to time we make our lists of customers available to reputable third parties who may have a product or service of interest to you. If you would prefer we not share your name and address, please check here. ☐

SDES09

# COMING NEXT MONTH
## Available November 10, 2009

**#1975 WESTMORELAND'S WAY—Brenda Jackson**
*Man of the Month*
After a mind-blowing night of passion with the raven-haired beauty, this Westmoreland has decided he's the man destined to satisfy *all* her needs....

**#1976 IN THE ARMS OF THE RANCHER—Joan Hohl**
A solitary ranch man, he agrees to a short-term marriage to shield her from her dark past. Yet as the time nears for the arrangement's end, their desire may be all too permanent.

**#1977 THE MAVERICK'S VIRGIN MISTRESS—
Jennifer Lewis**
*Texas Cattleman's Club: Maverick County Millionaires*
This tycoon has met the perfect woman. But when he offers her protection in his posh penthouse, will she discover their relationship is built on a lie?

**#1978 WEDDING AT KING'S CONVENIENCE—
Maureen Child**
*Kings of California*
When a night of passion leads to pregnancy, the film studio exec proposes a marriage of convenience. His bride-to-be, however, refuses to settle for anything less than love.

**#1979 CHRISTMAS WITH THE PRINCE—Michelle Celmer**
*Royal Seductions*
The island prince will show his reserved scientist how to have a little fun—outside the bedroom *and* under the sheets.

**#1980 HIS HIGH-STAKES HOLIDAY SEDUCTION—
Emilie Rose**
*The Hightower Affairs*
Forced to pretend a past relationship he never had for the sake of the company's reputation, this CEO finds himself caught in the middle of a passionate affair based on mistaken identity.

SDCNMBPA1009